THE

BOOK OF SHADOWS

ALSO BY RUTH HATFIELD

The Book of Storms
The Colour of Darkness

THE
BOOK OF
SHADOWS

RUTH HATFIELD

HOT
KEY
BOOKS

First published in Great Britain in 2016 by
HOT KEY BOOKS
80–81 Wimpole St, London W1G 9RE
www.hotkeybooks.com

A CIP catalogue record for this book is available from the British Library.

ISBN: 978-1-4714-0302-6
also available as an ebook

1

This book is typeset using Atomik ePublisher•
Printed and bound by Clays Ltd, St Ives Plc

Hot Key Books is an imprint of Bonnier Zaffre Ltd,
a Bonnier Publishing company
www.bonnierpublishing.com

To M.M.

They walk under the railway bridge, down on the old canal. They always walk there. Today it's hard and cold and the air is dead, and damp leaves are decaying in a slippery pavement over the towpath.

The golden dog lingers behind, sniffing at a pile of mud. She pushes her nose into it and breathes in deeply, inhaling the scent of dead beetles and slime. A good smell. The beetles might still be solid enough to crunch between her teeth.

She hovers, about to open her jaws and take a good bite, when a thin shadow of soft air brushes over her coat. A long-forgotten warmth stands close beside her.

She pulls her head back. The old man has wandered on – he tramps at a steady pace, trusting that she'll catch up, as she always does.

But standing next to her, is –

Someone else.

Someone she has been waiting for.

Tall and thin, with close-curled hair and eyes as dark as night, he puts out a hand to stroke her head. From inside his shirt collar a tiny brown head peeps up, chattering angrily.

He only smiles. 'It's time, dog,' he says. 'Time to go to your master.'

The golden dog looks up the towpath one last time. The old man trudges around a bend and disappears out of sight.

Their walk is nearly over. The old man is going home.

And the golden dog turns away, looking over the dank, green canal.

'It's time,' Sammael says again.

She looks up at him, and wags her tail.

Chapter 1

Into the Sea

They were there again.

Danny ducked behind a half-built boat and peered through the gaps in the planks. He'd thought seven would be early enough; that Paul and his cronies would still be in bed, or stuffing Coco Pops into their mouths and watching breakfast cartoons.

But even Paul wasn't going to spend his half term in bed, apparently. He was going to spend it being in exactly the places Danny wanted to be.

For a moment, Danny looked beyond the gang of boys down on the grey beach. He turned his eyes further out to the wide sea, flecked with white foam under a dour October sky. A gust of raw salt breezed across the endless water, bringing the smell of distance into Danny's nostrils. The smell of –

Adventure.

His hand trembled; he pushed hard against the boat in

a spasm of hope, and the boat toppled slowly sideways, off its wooden rest.

It crashed onto the hard standing at the top of the beach, and the gang of boys looked up. Danny didn't waste time trying to freeze in the hope they wouldn't notice him.

He ran, like a coward.

'There he is!'

'Get him!'

He kept to the concrete, hoping that the sand below would slow them, but they hadn't been far away, and within a few strides they were at the top of the beach and pounding after him – Paul, the captain of the Year 9 football team, and his friends – his newly made, holiday friends –

Danny's head jerked sideways as pain bit at his ear. Now they were throwing things. Stones. Shells. Flotsam and jetsam from the grimy beach.

And then he was hurdling the low wall around the hard standing, and there was only the beach path to run along, and the land to his left was sand and gorse and chips of stone, leading nowhere but down to the sea.

He had run the wrong way. He should have taken off back into town, run to the house of his parents' friends, knocked on the door and bolted inside.

'Go on! Get him!'

A stone smacked into the small of his back. Numbness shot down his leg, fizzing and popping. He couldn't swing it properly any more, could only run with an awkward limp. He hopped and skipped.

'Skipping like a girl! You're a girl, Danny O'Neill!'

If only he could run with his arms, like a monkey. He stumbled, pitched into a gorse bush, pushed himself free of the thorns and ran on without stopping to examine the angry red scratches along his arms that hissed out blood.

Another stone hit his back. He gasped, drawing burning air into his chest. But he didn't need to run so fast. They were just playing with him now. They were running him, like cowboys with a steer, herding him towards the edge of the sea. When he got there they would surround him, and there would be nowhere left to run.

Danny looked desperately to his right and left, hoping that the sands might throw up some help – a massive hole, maybe, or a rope that would zip up out of the beach like an enormous buried snake and throw its end into his hands so he could be dragged up into the sky as if he was hanging onto the tail of a giant kite.

There was nothing like that here, of course. Only the grey morning and the autumn chill picking at the wind.

He kept running even though there was no point, and then, a short way down the beach, he saw a little wooden boat in the shallows.

Waiting for him.

Perhaps it had come adrift from its moorings in the harbour and washed up here. Perhaps some magic spirit had taken pity on him and left it to aid his flight.

Either way, he doubled his pace and sprinted for the boat, and he heard them behind him, gathering themselves, seeing their prize suddenly slipping away. But he was far enough ahead, and he splashed into the shallows, leaping into the little boat and fumbling for the oars.

They were still in the rowlocks, neatly tucked across the seats. Danny swung them wide into the sea. Bracing his arms against the solid bulk of water, he took a pull and the boat glided away from the shore.

For a second, he felt as though the wings of an enormous bird had sprouted from his shoulders and he was beating them against the clear air, launching himself up into the sky.

He'd done it. He'd escaped them.

They stood on the shore, their dumb faces slack in disbelief. Paul threw a bit of driftwood, but the rising wind batted it back towards him, protecting Danny.

'Big fat girl!' Paul shouted.

Danny let himself smile, and kept pulling at the oars.

'We'll get you next time!' yelled one of Paul's goons.

There would be a next time, for sure. Once upon a time, Paul had been Danny's best friend. Then all the strange things had started to happen, and Danny had made the mistake of telling Paul. And it seemed as though Paul had been, through all their years of friendship, just a pile of toadspawn waiting to hatch out into a huge, warty, bullying toad.

'Just ignore him,' the teachers said. But how could you ignore someone when you went on holiday, miles and miles from home, and they turned up there too? Danny just wanted to explore the place and throw stones into the sea. Apparently that was too much to ask.

The wind hissed and the waves rose. The little boat toppled from wave to wave, throwing Danny's stomach around like a beach ball. He looked back towards the shore. It seemed impossibly far away. Paul and the others were drifting back to town, and the beach lay empty.

Without warning, a big wave hit the side of the boat, sending a cold spray of salt against the back of Danny's neck. He took a better hold on the oars, trying to steady himself. Already the sea felt too powerful.

There was no need to panic though. Out here, he had a weapon. He wedged the ends of the oars under his armpits and reached into his pocket, pulling it out.

The taro.

It was just a twig from a sycamore tree, brown-barked and smooth from handling, the size and shape of a pencil. But the taro had been the beginning of all the strange happenings. In summer, the previous year, there had been a storm. It had left behind a bolt of lightning, trapped inside a stick. And then, and then . . .

Danny forced himself to close his mind to all that other stuff. He shut his eyes and listened, following the sound of the waves from the bristling surface down into the dark depths of churning water, and he listened hard to the very heart of the sea. He had spoken to the sea before, a long way from here, and it had been wise and kind. Hopefully this would be the same sea.

When he could feel the sea's voice coating his mind, he said, inside his head, 'Sea? Sea, can you hear me?'

The sea flattened itself in one stretching gasp, and tiny waves prickled up like the hackles of an angry cat.

'Who calls on me? Who *dares* to call on me?'

It wasn't the same sea as last time. This sea had a voice like an elderly woman, frail and cracked with a core of steel.

'I need help,' Danny tried. 'I need to go back. Please . . .'

'A *human*!' the sea shrieked. 'How dare a *human* call on me for help?'

'Please . . .' Danny tried again.

'HOW DARE YOU?' it shrieked, in a voice as hard and thin as a rusted old spear. 'HOW DARE YOU EVEN TALK TO ME?'

'Sorry!' gasped Danny, as the flattened waves rose up in a terrifying wall of white water. 'Sorry – please – don't –'

The waves reared above his head and let go. They pounded onto the planks of the little wooden boat, filling it with water, pushing it downwards.

'Please!' choked Danny. 'I just want to get back – to land –'

'I DO NOT HELP HUMANS!' screamed the sea. 'I AM THE WIDOW-MAKER! THE DROWNER OF DREAMS! I AM THE MERCILESS SEA!'

And with that, white waves rose again out of the soft grey water, clawing up at Danny's little dinghy, throwing it into the air. The boat leapt like a plunging horse. For a moment Danny clung to the sides and thought: it's fine, I'm safe, I'll go up and come down again – and then the dinghy's prow was pointing towards the sky and the boat was tipping over his head, and he was tumbling into the freezing water.

He gasped. Salt and foam flew into his mouth. Panic clawed across his stomach and he kicked his feet down.

Nothing but water below.

'Please!' he yelled desperately. 'Please! Stop! Help!'

'HA!' yelled the sea, so loudly that the inside of Danny's head buzzed with salt. 'I don't help *anything*!'

Danny flailed out with his arms, clenched his fists – whatever he did, he couldn't lose the taro. He tried to swim, but his arms and legs had given up on him. He was going to slide under the rising waves and sink down into the cold sea, and instead of breathing in air, he would draw icy water into his lungs, and in a few moments it would all be over.

The waves curled up around him and pushed him down into the depths of the sea, and he could not resist them any more.

After seconds, Danny's lungs were burning. Pinpricks of colour swam up his vision, and dark shapes drifted in front of his eyes. Wisps waving from side to side, almost clear against the murky gloom of the sea. Plants? Seaweed?

The shapes grew larger, and hope surged in him. Chromos! The land of colours!

Once, he'd got to Chromos through the sea. He'd raced into the moonlit waves on the back of a stag and leapt into a fantastically changing world of dreams, and he'd raced through it, and come out again, breathing and alive –

But the pinpricks of colour were fading, and only the shapes were left, looming through the murky sea. Only one shape, in fact.

What was it?

Some kind of hair.

Hair, down here?

Blond hair.

Danny reached out and touched it. It was almost as soft as the numbing water. Was it attached to anything? He gave a gentle tug. Heavy, but not immovable. Solid, but not hard. He pulled again, using the last bit of his strength.

The object broke away from whatever had held it, and floated up in front of him, pale and gloomy.

A body.

He screamed, in soundless panic.

Bleach-white, the body straggled through the hazy water, limbs flailing. It was almost naked, with only a scrap of ragged cloth around one arm that might once have been a sleeve.

Danny tried to twist away, to swim in the other direction, but his own limbs were silent and still, and would not obey him.

Then the body rolled over in the shifting currents and he saw its face.

Familiar. As familiar as his own mum or dad. He knew this person.

But . . . who was it?

Someone pushed themselves to the front of Danny's head: his Aunt Kathleen, tall and bony, a farmer on a windswept hillside. But this body was a young man, only a few years older than Danny.

The body opened its eyes and stared at him. Even in the dark gloom, they were clearly blue.

The body's mouth smiled.

Danny forgot that he was drowning, and that he had only moments left to live. Fleshy white arms drifted out towards him. The mouth kept smiling.

He tried to push at it, but not even his own hands would listen to him. Dead skin brushed against his arm; a white hand emerged from the tattered sleeve and curled out fingers to fix around his wrist. The face came closer, pale and flabby, with lips as grey as rainclouds.

The mouth opened.

Danny closed his eyes, waiting for teeth to sink into his cheek. But he felt a touch on his face as soft as his mother's hand, and he dared to look again.

The body smiled, one last time, a smile as broad as the hills and fields around Aunt Kathleen's farm. And then it leant forward, and the opening of its mouth was black and fathomless.

For a second, Danny thought the mouth was going to get bigger and bigger until it swallowed him up. But he was wrong. Nothing was going in.

Something was coming out.

Bubbles.

They floated into his mouth, giving him a single, precious breath.

And then his head was breaking the surface of the water, and the waves were crashing all about him, and there was nothing to hold onto except for the salt of the sea, soft between his fingers. Danny reached out, sure that the dinghy must be somewhere close, but he swiped and swiped and grabbed and grasped and there was nothing.

Just as he was about to give up and let himself slide back down beneath the waves again, something warm and solid knocked against him, and this time it wasn't a body, drifting in eerie silence. It was a real, struggling, panting creature, striking out with four legs, keeping itself afloat and coming to his rescue.

A dog.

Not once did Danny ask himself what it was doing so far out to sea. Not a thought went through his head but that he should cling to it.

Danny clung to the dog, and together they swam for shore.

Chapter 2

Ori

Everything happened too fast. There was the dog's fur under his fingers, his hand clenched around it, never letting go, and there was the frenzied swim through the raging sea, and the gritty rising of the beach under his knees, and the thousand fragments of broken shell stabbing into his cheek as he lay panting, dragged up on the shore. Small waves grabbed at his ankles, trying to pull him back into the snarling water, but he'd come too far ashore; they couldn't get him now. He was safe, the dog's fur in one hand and the taro in the other.

Before he could think to speak, voices came, and running feet through the sand, and panic, anger –

'What the devil!'

'Is he – ?'

'Kids!'

And soft curses, hands turning him over. People peering into his face.

'Son? Son? You OK?'

13

'Who is he? Anyone know?'

'Damn tourists. Damn kids.'

'He's staying with Tony, down along. Dunno his name, though.'

'Damn kids.'

Danny blinked, tried to open his mouth to speak, but choked instead. Gulps of seawater scraped up his throat, and he mixed up swallowing and breathing. His lungs were scalded by sharp fire.

The dog struggled under his grip, and he realised his arm was as tight as iron around her.

'Don't go,' he said silently to the dog. 'Don't leave me.'

'Of course I won't leave,' said the dog. 'You're safe with me.'

But hands were separating them, pulling him away, and he was being lifted, cradled in rough-coated arms as the wind howled about the beach. The voices were grim and the footsteps hurried, and Danny could only clutch the stick and say silently to the dog, 'Don't leave. Please stay.'

And then Danny's world went blank, and he lost sight of them all.

He woke in the small bedroom he'd been staying in all week. The curtains were closed, though a weak daylight crept around the sides. A smell of frying fish and onions trickled along the sleeping air, and voices spoke softly in the room below.

Danny's head spun. He was standing on a high ledge above the world, looking down on it with nausea clawing at his stomach. He was losing his balance and something was standing just behind him, ready to help him fall . . .

No, he told himself. It's just the salt water in my stomach, making me feel sick. Nothing strange is happening at all.

Except –

And as soon as he thought about the taro, he knew it was still in his hand, still joining him to that other world of talking animals and raging seas.

There was something real, panting heavily, waiting for him in the darkness.

He craned his neck to look at her. The thin glow from the curtain edges told him that she was big and solid, and lying patiently beside his bed. Over the frying food smell, he recognised the scent of her: warm, thick and earthy.

'Are you there?' he asked, keeping the voice in his head very small, just to make doubly and triply sure that there was no chance whatsoever of the sea hearing him.

'Yes,' came the reply in the dog's warm voice.

Danny relaxed once he'd heard it. 'You saved my life.'

'Yes, of course I did. I saw that you were drowning. I swam out to you, so that I could guide you back to shore.'

A huge lump rose in Danny's throat, trying to force tears from his eyes. He managed to swallow before it overwhelmed him.

'Thanks,' he said. It seemed a very small thing to say.

'Don't mention it,' said the dog. 'I was looking for something to do, anyway. But how is it that you can talk so clearly to me? It is as though you have learnt the language of dogs.'

She had a voice that shone with sunlight. It made her sound as though she were always smiling.

Danny peered at her. A huge, curly-coated golden dog with a pleased face and deep eyes, she was sprawled on the floor, her chin on her paws. Her coat was matted with salt. Perhaps she was some kind of search and rescue dog.

He hesitated. Could he trust her with the truth?

'I'll tell you,' said Danny. 'But tell me first – who are you? I mean, who owns you?'

'Tsk tsk,' said the dog. 'You humans! I am Ori, and I own myself.'

'You're a stray?'

The dog tilted her head. 'Call it that if you like. I had an owner once, but life moves on.'

Ori seemed so casual. Cold, almost. But if she hadn't helped him, he wouldn't be lying in this little room with the smell of frying dancing up from the kitchen below. He'd be dead.

With a touch of shame at having doubted her, Danny told Ori about the taro.

'I found it under a tree,' he said. 'A sycamore tree. When I hold it, I can talk to anything.'

He didn't mention all the other stuff that had happened. Judging from Paul's reaction, it wasn't a good way to make friends.

'But if you can talk to everything,' Ori said, 'then why didn't you ask the sea itself to help you?'

'I did,' said Danny. 'The sea wasn't keen.'

The second he let himself think about the sea, it all came back to him.

16

The body under the waves.

So familiar.

Those bubbles – he saw them now, floating towards him through the dark, grey sea, pouring into his mouth. Ori might have pulled him back to shore, but the body had saved his life before that, by breathing oxygen into him.

It was impossible.

Perhaps he'd imagined it. Yes, that must be right. It was impossible and he'd imagined it.

Danny stared down the side of the blue-sheeted bed towards Ori on the varnished floorboards, and knew he hadn't imagined it. Plenty of things were impossible. Until they happened.

'Did you see anyone else in the sea?' he asked the dog.

She stared at him. 'There was someone with you? But I only saw you, in the boat. I saw you jump in when the other boys chased you. You were alone, weren't you?'

'Yeah,' Danny tried nodding, but it made his head swim. 'Yeah, there was only me. But I saw –'

He pulled himself up short. The strange stuff again. Would Ori react just like Paul, and laugh at him?

But as he looked at her warm eyes and soft face, he knew he could trust her.

'I saw a body,' he said. He didn't add the part about breathing. It sounded too silly.

'A dead body?'

'Well . . . yeah. I suppose so.'

'How sad. Probably a drowned sailor. He'll be washed ashore at the next high tide, somewhere along the coast.'

'No.' Danny shook his head. 'Not a sailor. I knew him.'

17

'You *knew* him?' Ori spoke sharply, scrambling to her feet. 'Then you weren't alone? I must go back and swim out again. Perhaps it's not too late.'

'It is too late,' said Danny, and an overwhelming pain rose up in his chest, squeezing hard at his lungs. 'I told you, he's dead.'

Ori came forward so that her head was within his reach, and for a long moment he clutched at the fur behind her ears, digging his hands into it for comfort.

A cloud of pictures came back to him. The summer just gone. Isbjin al-Orr, the stag. A girl called Cath Carrera and a hare called Barshin. Riding into the sea, into Chromos, into a wild, wild adventure trying to save someone – to save someone's life . . .

The memories coursed through his blood, as sharp as hot spice, and his skin tingled.

He clutched at the dog's fur in a spasm that sent his fingernails digging so deeply into his palms that one drew a tiny speck of blood, and as he unbent his fingers and saw the red spot on the dog's golden coat, he saw what had been missing from his memory.

Red and gold.

Flames.

There had been a fire, and someone had died. No, not just someone. He knew, now. The person who had died had been his cousin Tom.

And the fire had been started by –

Sammael.

Sammael, who belonged to the darkness. He hated Danny, and he had killed Tom to hurt him.

Now Tom was dead, and Danny –

Danny closed his eyes. Why hadn't his parents talked to him about Tom? They had kept a horrible conspiracy of silence, and let him forget. He shouldn't have been allowed to forget, not ever.

'I know who it was,' he said at last to Ori. 'And it's much too late.'

He told her all about the journey in the summer, and Tom's death, and Sammael.

'But Sammael's still around somewhere,' he said. 'I just took his boots off him, so he couldn't go into Chromos. He used to take dead people's souls through Chromos so they picked up the colours, then he'd put the souls into living people's heads, so they did awful things. I stopped him from doing that, but he's still alive somewhere. Probably making new boots. And Tom –'

'. . . Is dead,' said Ori gently, and Danny realised he'd said it about fifty times as he'd explained. And no matter how many times he said it, he couldn't budge the awful solidness of its truth.

'Knock knock,' said a voice, and the door opened. Danny's mum came in with a tray.

Danny stared at her as she smiled and put the tray on the bedside table. It had something that smelled warm and milky on it, but he didn't bother to look at what.

'How are you feeling, love?' She put her hand on his forehead for a moment, then brushed it back through his hair. 'You gave us all such a fright.'

He couldn't find breath enough to speak; a flood of fear and relief and anger swept over him as violently as the raging sea, and he took a deep gulp of air, fighting off tears.

His mum gave him a kiss, and looked at the golden dog.

'Where did you come from, eh?' she asked in a voice that was full of wonder.

'Do you know?' Danny croaked. 'Does she belong to someone?'

His mum shook her head. 'She escaped from the rescue centre in town. They found her a couple of days ago, wandering along the main road. That's all they know about her. We'll take her back, tomorrow.'

'No,' said Danny. He looked at Ori, waiting patiently with her salt-crusted fur, her friendly face. 'She saved my life. I want to keep her.'

'Well, we'll see,' said his mum. She picked up the bowl of food, about to offer it to Danny, but his arm jerked wildly towards it, pushing it away.

'Why didn't you tell me about Tom?' he burst out, struggling to sit up in the narrow bed.

His mum frowned. 'Sorry?'

'You didn't tell me that Tom died! Why didn't you tell me? You let me forget!'

'Tom? Who's Tom?'

He couldn't believe it. Was she still trying to pretend?

'Tom!' Danny tried to keep his cool. 'I've remembered about him. But none of you told me. You knew he was dead, and you've let me go on all this time thinking that he didn't even exist. Not even thinking! Just not knowing! It's horrible! Weren't you even sad? Isn't Aunt Kathleen even sad?'

His mum put her hand on his forehead, and he knew from the coolness of it that he was burning hot.

'Danny, love, you're not making sense. There's no one called Tom here.'

'No, I know! Not here! At the farm!'

'No one at the farm, either. I don't know who you're talking about.'

'Tom! My cousin!'

His mum shook her head. 'You don't have a cousin called Tom. Only one called Sophie. But you nearly drowned, love. Everything's mixed up in your head. Why don't you eat and then sleep till morning, and it'll all be clearer then. Tom's probably one of your friends. You just need some sleep.'

Danny opened his mouth to protest and a jet of salt spurted from his stomach into his mouth. It splashed out onto the pale-blue sheet and he stared at it for a moment, astonished at how swiftly it had appeared, and then it was followed by a cascade of water flowing from his mouth as smoothly as a spring from the spout of a gargoyle.

'Oh, love,' said his mum. 'Let's get you some dry sheets.'

He stood shivering while she changed them, the floorboards rough under his cold feet.

'Back into bed with you,' she said.

He fell back onto the soft pillows and down into a deep sleep.

They denied Tom again in the morning. No matter how much Danny insisted, neither his mum nor his dad would admit that Tom had ever existed. When he said he was going to call Aunt Kathleen, they took the phone off him and told him not to be silly.

They wanted to talk about Paul. Not to the extent of doing anything about him, of course. They wanted to help Danny 'deal with things'. By himself.

You're finding growing up very hard, they said. We know you are. You and Paul used to be such good friends. But you haven't any friends, now, have you? You only want to spend time on your own. It's not normal. You've got to join in, talk to people. You're at a difficult age. A confusing age. Everything changes. But you can't just give up.

He stared at them. How was it that a year ago they'd all known each other so well? He and his parents had liked each other, been happy together. And now they didn't seem to know who he was at all. And he couldn't imagine what was going on in their heads for them to say such daft things.

He didn't bother to repeat how Paul was making his life hell, and the only reason for it was that Paul was a nasty kid who enjoyed picking on others. He didn't even bother to protest when they suggested he join the Saturday football club at school, so that he could do 'something fun' with the other kids. They had obviously entirely forgotten how much he'd always hated PE.

He gave up trying to make sense of it all as they packed up at the end of the holiday and went home. But he clung to one thing, and he wasn't letting it go.

Ori was coming with him.

Chapter 3

Holes

Danny kicked his boots through the scurf of yellow leaves as he trudged towards school. Monday morning. Back for the half term until Christmas. Back for weeks and weeks of sitting in classrooms staring out of the window at the grey sky and trying not to react to the pellets of paper flung at the back of his head. He supposed he should fight. If he let Paul beat him up, perhaps that would end it. Perhaps he'd be left alone.

But it would hurt, a lot.

'You look miserable,' said Ori, trotting freely through the leaves, her golden coat pale under the brilliant blue sky. 'In fact, scratch that. You are miserable. Is it really just this boy Paul? I could come into school with you, you know. I could bite him for you. I'm not a naturally aggressive dog. He'd never see me coming.'

'Thanks,' said Danny. 'But it'd cause all sorts of trouble. And you'd get taken away and probably put down, or something. It's all just impossible.'

He stopped by the first plane tree of the line that led down to the school gates and leant against it, tucking himself in to avoid the stream of other school-bound children.

'Not impossible,' said Ori gently. 'I'll be here when you finish school. I'll wait for you. We can go somewhere fun.'

'It's not just Paul.' Danny shook his head to free himself from the knowledge of what waited inside the school gates. 'It's all that other stuff too.'

'Tom?'

'Yes! Of course Tom! I mean –'

He turned and ground his fist angrily into the rough bark of the tree. 'I mean – how can everyone – everything – just be going on, all normally? Tom's vanished, and everybody's pretending he never even existed! I can't –'

He broke off, because he'd been about to say, I can't bear it, and it seemed like an artificial thing to say – he could bear it, of course; the knowledge was sitting on his shoulders as though an elephant had draped itself around his neck. If he just moved his feet, he would carry the elephant into school, all through the day, and out of the other side into the evening. He would go through the motions of life, and he would bear it.

But the knowledge of Tom made him want to throw back his head and howl. His ears buzzed. Every step he took closer to school, the feeling grew stronger and stronger, and he knew that if he did sit all day in his classrooms, being good and trying to listen, all he would hear would be the buzzing and the desperate urge to howl. At some point he might actually start howling. And Paul would never let him live that down.

'What are you going to do?' asked Ori.

Danny shrugged.

'Well, are you going to school, or not?'

Danny shook his head. Her question freed him, somehow. He wasn't going to school. 'I've got to ask her.'

'Who?'

'My Aunt Kathleen. Tom's mum. She must remember him. At least if I hear someone else talking about him, I'll know I'm not going mad.'

'You're not going mad,' said Ori. 'It sounded very clear to me.'

'Someone's mad here, for sure,' said Danny. 'And I'm not going to find out anything by sitting in school.'

'Of course not,' agreed Ori. 'It looks like a bleak place. Although with an interesting scent.'

'Yeah. The smell of boredom and stupidity,' said Danny, kicking at the leaves again. Not caring at all if anyone saw him, he began to walk in the opposite direction, against the tide of navy jumpers and black trousers.

'Come on,' he called to Ori inside his head. 'I'm going to the farm. Right now.'

And he hardly saw the faces of the others who were walking towards school as they turned to look at him, wondering why on earth he was going the wrong way.

He used his dinner money to pay for the bus, which dropped him down in the nearest village. The road up to Sopper's Edge was narrow and rough, and the wind always seemed to pick up halfway along it, so that by the time Danny reached the driveway to the farm, his face was chafed and blue and his hands a blotchy red.

He jogged up the drive to try to get warm again, and every step brought upon him a more and more curious feeling – that this was a place he knew better than any except his own home – he even remembered the exact configuration of potholes, and the slalom a car had to swerve through to avoid them. He knew the names of all the fields along the drive, and the places where the cocksfoot and Yorkshire mist grew tall in the spring. But it was Tom who had given him all this knowledge, and Tom had disappeared. There was a hole in Danny's memory as wide as the farm itself.

Aunt Kathleen was dragging a wooden hurdle across the yard, her grimy overalls smeared with bright green lichen. She stopped when she saw Danny and heaved the hurdle onto her shoulder, flinging it onto a pile of broken junk and dusting off her hands.

'Danny! What are you doing here? Is it half term already?'

Danny swallowed. 'No. Last week.'

'You haven't skipped school again, have you?'

She finished brushing the lichen from her hands and took a swipe at her overalls. Danny watched the cloud of green dust. His aunt watched him.

Maybe she would mention Tom herself, if he waited long enough.

'Danny, are you OK?' Aunt Kathleen's toffee-coloured hair escaped from its ragged bun and flew across her face in the cold wind, whipping at her cheek.

'C-can I come in?' Danny's teeth chattered, chopping his words into fragments.

'Go in, of course, you know you don't have to ask. That's a nice dog. Where's she from?'

Danny escaped into the farmhouse, Ori at his heels. Stepping through the door, a thousand vanished Toms wailed at him: Tom's coat, gone from the hook; Tom's cap, gone from the chair in the hall; Tom's strewn litter of magazines and jumpers, gone from every other chair in the house.

Aunt Kathleen put the kettle on and plonked food down in front of Danny. Chocolate biscuits. Fruit cake. A lump of meat pie.

Grabbing the knife, he hacked off a chunk of pie and crammed it into his mouth, bringing back a sense of déjà vu so strong that his head spun.

In the summer, he'd been here with Cath Carrera. Then, it had been Cath Carrera, not him, cramming food into her mouth, and the three of them – Danny, Cath and Tom – had been in the kitchen, arguing about Tom's sand. Tom's sand – Tom's *soul* – that he'd given away to Sammael.

'It's a shame, it really is,' Aunt Kathleen was saying as she made the tea. 'And I'm worried they'll come up to Hangman's Wood. I'm making pit traps out of those old chicken coops. Give them a few broken legs if they do come.'

'What?' Danny cut another piece of the meat pie and shoved it into his mouth.

'The baiters. Badger baiters. I was saying, they've been seen over in Oak Stoveley. Do put that old coat on, Danny;

28

looking at you is making me feel cold. You're blue. Danny? Are you OK?'

Danny's hand had stopped just inside his mouth. He couldn't chew the pie any more. It was choking him. He began to gag.

Aunt Kathleen dropped the pot of tea, swept behind him and thumped him smartly between the shoulder blades. The pie came flying out of his mouth onto the table.

Danny gasped in a lungful of air. Badgers! Watching the badgers in the woods, Tom at his side, marching him cheerfully through the darkness, saying, 'They're great, really they are! Totally worth getting out of bed for, I promise! You just have to see them –'

There were so many things Danny would never have seen, if it hadn't been for Tom.

Ori looked up at him. Aunt Kathleen poured some tea and put it in front of him.

'Sip,' she said. 'Carefully.'

Danny sipped. He fed the spat-out meat pie to Ori, who ate it with dribbling enthusiasm. He looked around the farmhouse kitchen and saw, again, everything that was missing: the photos on the pin board, the model tractors, the poster of cow breeds by the cooker. This was the same room he'd known all his life. But every trace of Tom had vanished.

He put the tea down. 'Why didn't you tell me about Tom?' he asked.

Aunt Kathleen frowned. 'Who?'

'My cousin Tom. Your son.'

Aunt Kathleen shook her head gently.

Outrage surged, filling Danny's mouth with the taste of blood. He looked down at Ori, who was gazing at him with her soft black eyes.

'Danny, Tom's dead,' said Aunt Kathleen.

'I know,' said Danny. 'But none of you told me! Why did you let me forget?'

Aunt Kathleen frowned and sat down. 'There wasn't anything to forget,' she said. 'You never knew him. I had a son called Tom, but he died when he was just a tiny baby. It was a long time ago, before you were born. Has someone been telling you about him?'

'No, he was alive! He was alive . . . he was here last year. He went away this summer, when he was mending fences around Hangman's Wood . . . he went away because he'd found out how to talk to birds, and animals . . .'

'Danny! What are you talking about? We had a son called Tom, yes, but he died nearly eighteen years ago. It was two years before your sister died. He was born very ill, and he never came home to live here at all.'

'He did!' Danny ground his knuckles into the table. 'He lived for years and years and years, and we did loads of stuff together – he taught me everything I know about the farm, everything about going off and doing stuff on your own. It was Tom – I know it was . . .'

He trailed off as Sammael's words finally came back into his memory.

'All the memories of Tom belong to me. I can take them out of the earth so no one will remember that he was ever here. His mother will think she only has a daughter.'

30

And that's what he'd done. Somehow, Sammael had taken every clue to Tom's existence away. He had even carefully plastered over the cracks with false memories, like the one Aunt Kathleen was relating at this very moment.

It was clever.

It was awful.

Aunt Kathleen cut a slice of fruit cake and thought.

'You've always been an imaginative boy, Danny . . .' she said slowly.

'No I haven't,' said Danny.

'. . . And I understand that some very unsettling things have happened to you in the past year or so. You've probably felt very alone at times.'

Danny reached for Ori's golden fur, and clenched his hand around a fistful, being careful not to tug at the roots. He needed to hold onto something.

'What about the horses? Are they here? What about Apple?'

Surely the animals couldn't be as blind and dumb as the humans? Surely Tom's horse would have to remember the boy who had owned her?

Aunt Kathleen shook her head. 'The only horse we have is Sophie's old piebald pony, you know that. You always said we should name her, but we never did. She's too old to need a name now.'

But the piebald did have a name. She'd told it to Danny.

She was Shimny. She'd been at the farm for Tom's whole life, and he'd learnt to ride on her. Danny had learnt to ride on her, in a sort of way. Shimny was ancient and wise, and there was no way she'd have let Sammael mess around with her mind.

'I want to see her,' Danny said, getting to his feet.

Aunt Kathleen rose too. 'Fine,' she said. She wasn't the type to get hysterical, or start demanding that Danny talk sense. 'I'm going to ring your mum on the way, and get her to pick you up. You need to let us help you, Danny. You know we want to help.'

Ori bounded ahead as they went up the muddy track towards the high fields. The sky was pale and soft, and the clouds were drifting by.

'I'm glad your parents got you a dog,' said Aunt Kathleen. 'I've always told them that a boy needs a companion. They seemed to think that you wouldn't want to go out and walk the dog enough, but you're an outdoor sort of boy, aren't you?'

Danny didn't answer. It hurt too much – Tom had been the outdoorsy one. Aunt Kathleen was putting the things that had been her own son into the shape of her nephew. It was all a lie.

The sounds of the farm were all where they should be, around him. Sheep in the far fields, cows in the near ones. Birds in the trees, traffic on the road, wind in the hedge-twigs. Yes. All present and correct. Except Tom's voice: that belonged beside them.

Shimny was grazing in the topmost paddock. Her winter coat was thick and matted with mud, and her back was as dipped as a crescent moon. Quite how old she was, Danny had never dared ask.

'Here,' Aunt Kathleen handed him an apple. 'Bite pieces out of it for her. She can't manage a whole one these days.'

Danny approached the pony, one hand on the stick in his pocket.

'Hello,' he said.

The pony raised a black and white head to stare at him, long and hard.

'I wondered when you'd be back,' she said. 'What do you want me for now? You must know I'm too old to run.'

'I don't need you to run, it's OK. I just want to know what you remember about Tom.'

The old horse didn't react to the name. There was no twitch, no sudden start of recognition. 'Tom who?'

'Tom,' tried Danny again. 'My cousin. He used to ride you, remember? And then I did, and we went on that long ride, and got chased by dogs . . .'

'I recall that long ride perfectly, thank you,' said Shimny. 'You got chased by dogs. I had the misfortune to be carrying you on my back at the time.'

'Yes, yes!' said Danny, a spark of excitement picking at him. 'And Tom was with us, remember? On Apple? And you said she was silly, and she was, dancing around at everything. Don't you *remember*?'

The old horse lipped gently at his pockets in search of more treats and, finding none, gazed at him.

'We were alone, on that ride. You and I. Of course I remember. You could speak to me. It wasn't a thing I'd ever thought would happen, between a boy and a horse. But you spoke to me, and I took care of you and brought you safely home.'

'Don't you . . . ?'

But Danny stopped himself. What was the use? Sammael had clearly got to Shimny, too. Danny could quiz and quiz her all day, and he wouldn't be able to jog her memory. There were no memories of Tom left to jog.

Somehow, the sea had given Tom back to Danny. But only to Danny.

He raised his eyes to the hilltop and saw Tom, alive again, striding down the field to greet them. It was a vision so strong, so impossible to deny, that he turned to Aunt Kathleen and Shimny, his mouth open, about to point out the figure, to challenge them to name it.

But Aunt Kathleen was giving the old horse a pat, and their heads were bent together. And Danny knew that if he told them to look up the hillside, neither would know exactly where they were supposed to look.

His mum came up the track towards them, her brown hair neatly tied back, her thin face a tidier echo of Aunt Kathleen's wide. bony one. She was sighing.

'Danny, you can't,' she said. 'You have to go to school. I know it's hard, but you have to go.'

'She's lying too!' shouted Danny, because the wind was there to take his noise away, and he wanted to blast all their eardrums off. 'You're lying! She's lying! I know Tom was here – we did so much stuff – why can't you just admit it . . . ?' And he broke off, because he knew he wasn't making sense. They weren't lying. They really didn't remember Tom. Nobody remembered Tom. Sammael had taken all the memories of Tom away from the world, and only Danny remembered him now.

34

It was a kind of torture.

He's trying to make me go mad, thought Danny. He can't kill me, so he's trying to make me go mad.

But I won't go mad. I'll think of some way to make them all remember. I don't know how, but I'll do it, and then I'll have won.

'Danny,' his mum was saying. 'I'll take you back to school. Let's go and have a chat with one of your teachers. I'm sure we can sort this out.'

And although at any other time he would have died at the thought of his mum going with him to talk to the teachers about his problems, he found he didn't really care now. He let himself walk beside her, down the track and into the car, with Ori jumping into the back seat behind him, and he didn't protest at all.

He was thinking.

How could he do it? How could he persuade them that a person had once existed, when there were no photographs or belongings to prove he had? And when they wouldn't take Danny's word for it, because they thought he was inventing stuff to get out of school?

He would have to be very clever.

Even cleverer than the creature who had done this.

'You need to fit in,' said his mum, with a sympathetic smile.

No, I don't, thought Danny. I need to get out of here. I need to find Sammael again, and this time I need to kill him.

Chapter 4

The Shadows

It has begun.

The creature uncurls the thin black patch and lies it gently down on the grass.

A soft autumn sun breaks through the clouds, peering down with a lemon-coloured ray of sunshine onto the wide field. Nothing unusual there: a few sheep nibbling at the coarse grass, snug against the November air in their thick fleeces. A few houses dotted around, some cars on the road. Not much wildlife; most of it hiding out of the cold, damp day.

Except – what's that? That creature, far down in that field, standing next to –

The sun's ray gives a brief prod at the black patch and recoils as swiftly as a snail's horn.

The clouds snap shut.

A low rumbling gathers and the sky begins to shudder, straining to free itself from a strange hold. But all its normal lightness has gone: it freezes and shakes, seized with fear.

And then the white drains from the clouds, and they turn grey.

They bunch together, closer and closer, until all the clouds in the surrounding sky are huddled in one tight clump, and although far in the distance the sun still shines, the field and the sheep and the houses are entirely covered by shadow.

Green turns grey.

Blue turns grey.

Brown turns grey.

The sheep stop eating and hang their heads, blades of half-chewed grass dropping from between their slack lips. People in the houses put down their cups of tea and stare down at their chests, their hearts turned to stone. The leafless skeletons of the trees fade to a dull, powdery grey.

The only creature still moving in the landscape is the creature that has laid down the black patch. It takes a single, crazed look around the lifeless land and cackles to itself, twitching its legs in a shudder of delight.

'So easy! So easy! Just like that, and it's all gone . . .'

The creature lifts the black patch tentatively, a little afraid that dislodging the patch might dislodge its hold on the shadows, but although the clouds shake, nothing moves apart from the patch itself.

As if tasting a fine biscuit, the creature raises the patch to its lips and bites off a chunk, then spits it onto the ground.

The patch is laid to rest again, and the clouds once more become heavy and still.

The bitten-off mouthful of black begins to grow. It stretches and reaches out, losing the marks of the teeth that have severed it, and reforms into another wide, thin patch, almost exactly the same size and shape as the original one.

So it is true. Shadows beget shadows. Bite a piece off, and it will turn into a copy of its own original self.

This shadow is infinite, and in time it will suck the colour from the whole world.

The creature rolls it up and, holding tightly to the great prize, runs swiftly in the direction of the sunlight.

At last.

At last.

It has begun.

Chapter 5

Grey

'Watch out!'

'Ooof!'

Danny's head spun as the ball slammed against his cheek, sending muddy grass flying into his eye and spit spinning out of his mouth. It smarted, as if a cold, wet fist had swung at his face.

He'd grown used to not reacting. His face stung as he stood still and put fingers up to his cheek to check that the wetness wasn't coloured by blood.

'Danny!' The football coach came jogging up. 'For God's sake, watch the game! Are you on this field? Are you even on this planet?'

Danny shrugged.

'Let's have a look.' The coach yanked Danny's hand away and had a quick look, jabbing his thumb into the bruise. 'No harm done. Go and stand out for a minute. No, make that ten minutes. Your side won't miss you.'

Danny freed his head from the coach's grip and wandered over to the side of the field, as far away from the school as possible. Stupid football practice. What a waste of a Saturday morning.

'Looking a bit *wet*, Danny! Been in the sea again, have you?'

It was Paul, so stunningly brainless that he couldn't even think up good insults. Danny didn't bother to look over. Instead, he turned away from the game, glad to be rid of it. The last brown leaves still clung to the twigs of the hedge, shining in the weak sunlight. Grass, beetles and mud lay before him: they were better than football, any day.

He was watching an ant trying to grapple with a piece of leaf when he heard the sound.

His ears went cold.

Everybody else on the playing field was watching Paul, who had the ball on the right wing and was racing towards the goal furthest from Danny. Nobody was looking at the school buildings beyond, or the sky.

Nobody saw how the sky was shivering.

Nobody saw the distant clouds running towards them, casting the edge of their shadow first over the school buildings, and then over the corner of the playing field.

Nobody except Danny.

He watched, frozen for a few moments, as the sunlight was extinguished. As the light went, so did the colour.

The red faded from the bricks of the school buildings. The small patches of grass between the paths lost their shine, and the green dissolved into the air. Even the concrete paths darkened and dulled.

Everything went grey.

This is it, Danny thought. This is Sammael. He's found out that I've been using the stick to talk to Ori. This is his final revenge.

As the cloud shadow crawled over the football field, Paul slowed his run and came to a stop, letting the muddy grey ball dribble off over the back line. He stood facing the goalkeeper. They stared at each other.

Danny's trainers seemed as heavy as stone. He pulled at his feet, sure that they wouldn't move, but they lifted easily, light and bouncing, and before he could think, he was running away from the rumbling shadow as fast as his legs would take him.

If only he had a bike, or a horse – but there was a gap in the hedge at the back of the field, not far from where he'd been standing, and he kinked through it, out onto the footpath, taking a second glance back over his shoulder.

The cloud came to a grinding halt just before the hedge.

He ran a couple more paces backwards, just to check. The shadow didn't move. He, Danny O'Neill, was standing in the winter sunlight, and only a hundred metres away his teammates were hanging their heads or sinking to their knees on the football field, wandering aimlessly in a sea of grey paths and grey grass at the back of grey school building.

What on earth had just happened?

Danny took another step backwards. Faint birdsong twittered in the air behind him, still lit by weak sunshine, but no sounds floated up from the school. The whole playing field was grey and numb.

Things moved. But their colour had died. The white of the sky, the reds and blues of the football kits, the greens and browns Danny had been staring at in the long grass – dozens and dozens of them – had vanished in an instant and turned to grey.

He took a step forwards, and then forced himself to turn away. His skin tingled, telling him to turn back, to look closer. You'll never know what something is until you get close up and look at it, the tingling said. Didn't you learn that from last time?

But another tingling came, right between his shoulder blades, and it said another, simpler thing.

Danger. This is Sammael. Run.

Ori. He had to get Ori, before the shadows got to his house. And his parents, too – he had to get them all to safety.

Danny ran.

He ran towards the centre of town, trying to keep his tired legs from slowing, but as he rounded the corner of the street that led to the market square, he saw that he wasn't running fast enough.

The market square was already grey.

Crashed cars and buses lay about the streets, their engines quiet. Rubble piled up where they had crashed into buildings. The brightly coloured awnings of the market stalls had faded into grey and sagged on their broken props above grey tables bearing grey cabbages, grey sausages and grey bread. Grey pigeons wandered aimlessly about, their sharp eyes clouded over with mist.

Here, too? How many shadows were there? What if Danny's home was already gone? It would surely have been the first place Sammael would have attacked.

Of course it would.

Danny's shoulders sank. Everything was lost already. He might as well walk into the market square and take his place with the morose pigeons, or copy the woman at the cheese stall and fall face-first into a plate of Brie.

He was almost stepping forward to join the greyness when a sound from behind him made him turn. It took him a moment to identify it, because it was so out of place here, in the middle of town, on a concrete pavement. But when he looked down, black eyes bulged up at him.

A frog was squatting in the middle of the pavement. Staring at Danny, it croaked again, and hopped a few inches towards him. It surely couldn't have followed him here – he had been running faster than a frog could ever hop.

The frog croaked again, throat twitching. And Danny saw, with sudden clarity, that he didn't need to pull the stick out of his pocket and talk to it. The frog wasn't saying anything to him: it didn't know who he was. It was just here, and it was breaking a spell.

He had stared into the grey, and the grey had told him to give up hope, and he had believed it. Sammael was trying to play tricks with his mind.

Ha! You can't get me that easily! Danny stamped his foot in a way that reminded him suddenly and sharply of Cath

Carrera, and also sent the frog diving off the kerbstone into the road.

He raced back down the street, looking up at the sky to follow the edges of the cloud. The people just outside the shadows were gathered in bunches, staring at the grey, shuffling closer.

Danny clenched his jaw and kept running. He ran past prams and pushchairs abandoned on the cold pavements, old women fallen and helpless on the ground. Broken glass, broken cars and bicycles. The people were zombies. The cats were zombies. The dogs and the leafless trees were zombies. Nobody cared about themselves or anybody else.

He turned into his own street and saw the shadows gathering at the far end. In front of him were the neat pavements he saw every morning and afternoon, and the garden gates – brown, black, blue, yellow – and the green hedges and trees, shrubs and flowers.

'Ori! Mum! Dad!'

Ori came with a woof and a bounce, leaping over the front gate and landing heavily on the pavement. It gladdened Danny's heart to see her, glowing and lively, bounding to greet him.

'The shadows!' he gasped, pointing up towards the sky. 'Mum! Dad! Quick, come on!'

But they didn't come. Perhaps they couldn't hear him. He'd left them in the garden, gathering up rubbish for a bonfire. Only an hour ago. It seemed eternal.

Danny ran around the side of the house and clattered through the gate. The trees were waving in the breeze, the leaves were dancing down from the thinning branches. Everything was alive, full of –

His parents were still gathering sticks for the bonfire.

'Mum! Dad!' he called to them. 'Come on! Quick! We've got to get out of here!'

His dad stopped and dropped the armful of twigs onto the ragged lawn. 'Danny? Why aren't you – ?'

'Quick!' Danny beckoned wildly. 'Come on!'

They ran with him, back around the side of the house, out of the front gate, into the street.

'What is it?' asked his dad.

'The shadows!' Danny waved his hand towards the sky, towards the galloping shadows.

His dad stopped. His mum collided with his dad.

'Come on!' Danny tugged at their arms, but they stood still, smiling.

'It's OK, love. It's only a storm. We don't chase storms any more. We gave that up, remember?'

'No!' said Danny. 'I'm not chasing it! It's chasing us!'

'Oh, love,' said his mum, sighing. 'I know you don't like football, but give it a chance.'

'No!' screamed Danny, yanking at their hands. He might as well have been yanking at concrete bollards.

The clouds swept down the street, devouring the houses one by one. The edge of the shadow gulped over the chimney next door, and Danny tried one last time.

'Come on!'

'Oh, there's no point,' said his dad, and Danny looked at his dad's face, and it was grey.

He let go of their arms, turned, stumbled and fell forward, and as he put out his hands to break his fall, his fingertips reached into the shadow.

It was freezing. The cold ran down his arms as swiftly as pain, shooting towards his heart. A flash of agony shot through his brain – it had got him! The shadow was devouring his whole body –

And it stopped. Something stayed warm inside him: a small, hard voice that roared with fire.

He pushed himself up and took the stick from his pocket. It was hot in the palm of his hand. He had never truly understood what the stick had done to him, but there was no doubt that at the moment, it was doing its best to protect him from the grey despair of the shadows.

'Mum? Dad?' he bellowed, but it was no good. His parents had turned away and were staring at the road, and his words merely echoed back to him, bouncing off the lifeless brick walls.

His parents had been swallowed by the grey, and he was alone.

It wasn't the first time, Danny thought bitterly. He was always the one who had to carry on alone, standing strong against the dangers.

Except this time, he had Ori, golden at his heels.

'Run!' she shouted, leaping and barking. 'Run, now! They're still moving!'

Without thinking, Danny turned on his heel and ran, rounding the corner onto the main road. Ahead of him, the bus to Hailsbridge was pulling into the bus stop, and he sprinted towards it, fishing in his pocket with his free hand for some change. Damn! He was still in his football kit, and the taro was the only thing he had.

He leapt onto the bus, and Ori followed him.

'Please!' he gasped to the driver. 'I haven't got any money, but I've got to get away! The shadows!'

The driver stared at him through yellow-tinted glasses.

'Off you trot, sonny,' he said. 'And take your pooch with you. I don't give free rides.'

'No! I've got to go! It's all the –' he bit back the word 'shadows' – 'it's all that *stuff*! We've got to get out of here!'

The driver put his bald head on one side and considered Danny for a moment so long and agonising that Danny hopped from one leg to another, and knew how mad he must look. But maybe being mad would work in his favour.

'Reckon there have been a few crashes today, from my radio. Weather, isn't it? You need to go to a hospital?'

'No!' said Danny. The hospital was back in town. 'Just away! It's coming to get us!'

'Where're your parents, sonny?' the driver tried, but he glanced at his watch, and Danny knew he was giving up. Time to play crazy.

'They're on a rocket!' he burbled. 'They went to the moon, in the stuff! That's where we've got to go!'

The driver closed the bus door. 'Right, son. You sit up the front here where I can see you, and you keep a tight hold of that mutt. And I'll take you to the moon. Sound fair?'

'All the way?' Danny tried to sound amazed. 'Really?'

'All the way. And on schedule, too, if you'll sit down and let me get a move on.'

The bus driver let off his brake with a hiss. Danny sank into the seat and pressed his nose to the window, craning his head to watch as the shadow rolled up the street in their wake.

Why was nobody else watching it? How were they all so *blind*?

Hailsbridge was beyond Sopper's Edge. He could get off the bus and run up to Aunt Kathleen's farm, and warn her about the shadows. Aunt Kathleen was sensible, and she listened to him. She would know how to get Danny's parents to safety, and then he could begin trying to track down Sammael.

He shivered. Stupid football kit, making him cold.

Ori laid her head on his knee, and the warmth from her golden body began to thaw him.

Chapter 6

The Great Plain

'That was my fault, wasn't it?' said Danny.

'No, of course not,' said Ori. 'Why would it be?'

'I've been talking to you. Using the stick. Sammael knows it, and he's trying to scare me with these shadows. The stick was the whole problem in the first case – it's why he hates me. He knows I can talk to everything and find out stuff about him.'

'I only know the same stories about him as every other dog. And so many will be hurt by those shadows,' said Ori, shuffling closer to Danny's bare legs. 'From the legends I know, Sammael wouldn't lay waste like that.'

'Well, your legends are wrong,' said Danny. 'He wanted to kill all the humans in the world with a great storm when I first learnt about him. This is exactly like him, believe me.'

'But . . .' Ori lowered herself to the floor and sighed gustily as the bus bounced over a crack in the road. 'Surely Sammael is a creature of colours, not shadows?'

'What do you mean?' Danny shivered.

'I mean, those shadows are hopeless. They are the weapon of a creature without hope. In the stories told by dogs, Sammael is always making mischief, not pointlessly destroying everything.'

'It must be Sammael,' said Danny. 'What else could do that?'

Ori was quiet for a few minutes as the bus sped out of town. At last, changing tack, she said, 'What happened to your cousin Tom in the end, exactly? After he died, I mean.'

'I don't know,' said Danny. 'Well, I don't . . .'

He did know, though. It hadn't all ended with Tom dying. He had seen Tom again afterwards, or at least he'd seen Tom's body.

He summoned up the memory.

'Sammael took Tom to his home in the aether,' he said. 'He put him down outside his cave and then we made the moon burn the aether and Sammael chased us. He got stranded on Earth after that, so he never went back to collect Tom's sand.'

'And Tom is still there? In the aether?'

'I guess.'

'So not alive. But not yet finished with dying,' said Ori, getting to her feet and putting her paws on the seat so she could stare out of the window at the sun-dappled countryside.

Danny waited for her to say something else, but she didn't.

'So?' he said at last.

Ori took her paws off the seat and looked at him. 'The shadows are something to do with hopelessness,' she said.

'And what's more hopeless than a dead soul that belongs nowhere?'

Danny's heart contracted into an angry knot. He opened his mouth to deny it, to tell her she was mad and wrong. The shadows couldn't come from Tom, because it was half Danny's fault that he'd been left so carelessly in the aether, and that would mean that the shadows were really Danny's fault, too.

But it did make sense. And it was Sammael who'd made sure that Tom was neither alive nor dead; Sammael had taken his soul and left it lying on the ground. Even if the shadows came from Tom, the reason for them could still be traced back to Sammael. It was a clear and simple explanation, and once he'd thought about it, it seemed obvious to Danny.

'You really think,' he said, croaking on his words, 'that this could be Tom? Doing all this?'

Ori cocked her head to one side. 'It struck me as a possibility, that's all,' she said.

Danny knew that it was more than a possibility. It explained why he'd seen Tom's body under the water, why he'd begun to remember Tom.

Tom was back, and he was getting his revenge.

'I've got to get to him,' said Danny. 'I've got to put him back where he should be.'

'With Sammael?'

Danny shook his head. 'There's only one place Tom belongs. Back in the earth. I've got to give Tom back to the real Death.'

'Well, you should certainly try,' agreed Ori. 'Perhaps if you do, and the shadows go, then you'll know they did come from him.'

'It must be him,' said Danny. 'But at least I can do something about it, now I know.'

The bus began to slow, and he got ready to run.

'Danny! Not again!'

Aunt Kathleen was chucking forkfuls of slimy straw into a wheelbarrow by the hen house. She shook her head and jabbed the fork into the ground, leaning on it.

Danny slid to a halt in front of her, his teeth chattering.

'What's happened now? Where are your parents?'

For a second he couldn't answer, because the words couldn't defeat his ragged breath, and Ori was moving swiftly around his legs, waving her plumy tail in agitation, and he had to keep looking at the sky. It was white every time he glanced up, but he was sure the clouds were starting to shiver. He pushed his arm up, waving, hoping that she'd magically know already about the shadows.

Aunt Kathleen understood the same thing as his parents had.

'Have they gone again? Are they chasing a storm? I told them . . .'

But that was old news. Danny shook his head vigorously, shaking life back into his lungs.

'No! It's real! The sky – the clouds – the shadows –'

'Shadows? What are you talking about?'

'Come on!' He tugged at her grimy sleeve. 'We've got to get out of here!'

Aunt Kathleen removed his hand firmly from her wrist. With an exaggerated spread of her fingers, she closed her own hand around his, holding him tightly.

'Right,' she said. 'You tell me where to go, and we'll go together.'

With the other hand, she fished her phone from her pocket and pressed a couple of buttons.

'They won't answer,' said Danny. 'They've gone grey. We've got to get Shim— the pony – and get out of here! Far away!'

'Right. The pony,' said Aunt Kathleen. 'Yes, let's go and see the pony.'

She let the phone keep ringing, but of course his parents didn't answer.

'Are you sure they haven't gone chasing storms?' she asked, when they were halfway up the track to Shimny's field.

'I told you. They've gone grey.'

'Mmm,' was all that Aunt Kathleen said to this.

It was a shame. Aunt Kathleen had always been reasonably good at listening to him, not just assuming he was making up childish stories. But apparently even Aunt Kathleen's reasonableness had a limit.

The grip of her hand was comforting, though. When she let go of Danny at the gateway to Shimny's field, he felt a cold rush of air surround him.

Shimny was by the gate, staring off to the far hills, lip drooping. She raised her head as he approached, and for a second, he thought she was looking at him.

But she was staring at the sky.

'It was time for them,' she said. 'It was time for them, and they came.'

And he realised that while he had stopped listening, taking comfort in Aunt Kathleen's hand, the world had gone silent.

He whipped around. The cloud shadow was already at the bottom of the hill, racing up towards Sopper's Edge. This time, the air echoed before him, a wide ball of silence bouncing from cloud to cloud, sending darts cutting through the last trails of birdsong, snipping down the remaining gusts of wind.

'Run!' he shouted to Aunt Kathleen.

'Danny . . .' his aunt tried, but Danny was pointing at the clouds, at the grey, at the shadow running over the choking land.

'Run, before it gets here!'

Shimny tossed her head, snorting as he grabbed at her tangled mane.

'Oh no!' she said. 'I've done my running!'

Danny didn't listen. He knew better than any of them. Those who didn't run would go grey, and he couldn't bear to lose them – Shimny, Aunt Kathleen. They would just have to trust him.

He leapt up onto Shimny's back. It wasn't anything like the struggle it'd once been; he'd grown so much taller since the summer before last. He held out a hand to Aunt Kathleen.

'Get up! We've got to go!'

'Danny!' she protested. 'Come down from there. Come inside. We'll have tea.'

'Look!' He jabbed his finger towards the shadow, galloping now, up the hillside, eating up the front fields, swallowing the front yard.

'It's only cloud shadow, Danny. You always see it run up the farm, when you look at the view from here. Come down, now.'

'IT'S NOT A CLOUD SHADOW!' Danny screamed, his heart battering at his chest like the hammer of a bell. 'IT'S TOM!'

And it was the truth, the terrible truth. He knew it. The shadow was the shadow of Tom's torment, and it had somehow reached the land of Tom's farm and Tom's mum, and it was about to swallow both up in its anguish. Even the pony Tom had loved would fall into grey, along with every stick and stone and tree he had lived for. Perhaps he would find peace after that

Danny didn't think so. What peace could be found from destroying the things you had loved?

'Danny!' shouted Aunt Kathleen, as though a great wind had whipped up and was whirling away at the words that escaped from her mouth. 'Come down off that horse! Tom doesn't exist!'

Her hand flew to Shimny's neck, and her words echoed through the silence. There was no wind to shout over now. There was no sun to blind them, or rain to drive in their faces.

There was a still, wordless hillside, and nothing moved, and under the devouring shadows, the world turned swiftly grey.

Danny clenched his fist around the stick in his pocket. If only he could listen to the clouds – but these clouds were saying nothing. The only voice he could hear was his own, raging and furious.

He drove his heels into Shimny's sides. 'Run!' he yelled at her. 'Run for your life!'

Ori leapt at her side, but still, the horse wouldn't move. Danny felt the growing urge to turn back, to gaze into the shadows. If he threw the stick away and stepped underneath them, he would know what it was like, feeling all the last bits of joy and fear and hope drain from him, until nothing mattered any more.

He fought the pull with every last memory in his mind. All the wonderful things he'd done – those mad adventures: stags and seas and swallows in flight. And he looked ahead, to where the top of the hillside was green, with Hangman's Wood growing black and thick along the crest, and he put a vision of the great plain of Chromos over all of it.

The sky was a deep blue and the coarse hill grass sparkling emerald, and Shimny was not an old piebald pony, she was Zadoc, the great Guardian of Chromos, whom Danny had last ridden as a ghost, flying weightless over the great plain.

This time, he barely touched his heels to Shimny's sides. But the horse leapt forward as if stung by a wasp, or by the lash of Danny's hope. She put her head down and charged up the hill with Ori leaping beside her, and Danny's long legs wrapped around her sides. She jumped the fence out of the field and onto the track, and made for Hangman's Wood

Danny risked one last glance over his shoulder, and saw Aunt Kathleen's hand fall to her side. Her toffee-coloured hair and the weather-beaten red of her face faded to grey, and her head tilted towards the ground. But Shimny began leaping over hollows in the track, and he had to turn and concentrate on keeping himself balanced before he saw any more.

He did not need to watch to see Aunt Kathleen fall to her knees and sink face-forward into the mud. He felt a tearing pain in his heart, and he knew it had happened. And he could only promise to the rushing air and the scrubby grass and the thudding of Shimny's flying heels that he would be back in time to save her.

Chapter 7

A Bargain with Death

They ran until they broke out into the clear yellow sunshine of late afternoon, and the fading light spoke only of the natural ending of day. Hangman's Wood had disappeared far behind them; they were in countryside Danny didn't recognise. Ori was panting so hard that her body lurched with every breath.

Shimny came to a halt, tripping over her hooves and sinking to her knees. Danny leapt from her back and tugged at her mane, trying to get her to rise again. The horse didn't look as exhausted as the dog: her nostrils were stretching to suck in air, but her flanks were only gently blowing in and out. Still, she refused to get up.

They were on a road at the bottom of a shallow valley, and although Danny couldn't see beyond the low hills to the north and south, his view was broad and far-reaching. If the shadows came there would be plenty of time to react, as long as he kept his wits sharp.

He knelt on the cold road, cradling Shimny's heavy head in his lap for a moment and stroking her cheek. Her eyes were closed. Danny wasn't alarmed. She was just a little out of breath: she'd recover in a minute or two. Tough old horse.

Ori came to stand beside him, her long pink tongue hanging from her jaws. He took hold of the stick in his pocket.

'The shadows are bad,' she said.

Danny nodded. He felt Tom everywhere about him now – in the earth, in the wind and especially in the shadows. 'I know it's Tom,' he said. 'He's all around me, like the whole air is made of ghosts. He's not letting me forget any more.'

'Can't we go to him?'

Danny looked up at the darkening sky. 'I don't know how to get there. The only ways I know to the aether are through the moonlight on the sea, or through Chromos. And to get to places in Chromos, you have to want to get there, and to think hard about where you're going. I never knew how to think of the aether so that I could get there by myself – Cath was always with me. She was the one who knew what to do.'

'Where's Cath, then?' asked the dog, sitting down alongside Shimny's steaming bulk, either to steal the horse's warmth or to lend it some of her own.

Danny shook his head. 'I don't know. Well, I know that she's in a little house next to the sea, but we got there through Chromos, too. I've no idea how to get there on earth.'

'Well then,' Ori said, simply. 'We must go to Chromos, mustn't we? If you don't know the way to the aether, the only thing to do is to go and ask this Cath. Don't you think so?'

Danny's heart leapt into brightness. Of course they should find Cath. Cath was brave and strong. She would take him by the hand and her strength would flood through him, and the way forward would be clear.

And Chromos – when he'd come home through Chromos, that last time, on Zadoc's disappearing back, he'd raced over the great green plain and seen how wide the world was, how endless its possibility. He'd believed in himself. He'd believed he could do anything. If he went back to Chromos, he might be able to feel like that again.

But darkness crept inside him. There had been other times in Chromos. Times of terror. It had taken him several attempts to learn how to leave his fears behind him and travel with hope. Now, he saw that the lesson had only been a temporary one. Right now, he was afraid of the shadows, afraid of how much he was to blame for them. If he went to Chromos this night, he would take all the old hopelessness and fear with him, and it would come alive in there.

The light grew dimmer and a damp chill set into the air. Eventually he had to tell Ori the truth.

'Chromos was amazing, but . . . it frightened me,' he said. 'I wasn't good at travelling in there.'

'But surely that doesn't matter?' said Ori. 'We have to do it, don't we? I'll be with you.'

'It doesn't work like that,' said Danny, and despair kicked numbly at his shoulders. 'You have to *want* to go to Chromos. And once you're in there, you see what's strongest in your mind. I saw good things sometimes, but right now

60

I'm scared, so I'd just see all the things I'm scared of. I'm a coward, and Chromos knows that.'

'I see,' said Ori, thoughtfully, and was silent for a while, as the evening shadows grew long around them and the night drew in.

Danny stared hard at Shimny's sweat-soaked coat, stroking her crinkled hair flat and pressing it down to her neck. Goosebumps prickled on his arms.

He wanted to howl.

The dog dipped her golden snout and nudged at his arm, huddling closer to him. 'You're not all coward, you know. When I first met you, you nearly drowned. The next day you were back on your feet. And you don't fear the sea, do you?'

'No.' Danny shook his head. He didn't fear the sea, it was true. Whenever he thought of the sea, he still thought of riding Isbjin al-Orr into the waves, and the stag's power and strength and shining happiness. 'But I *am* scared in Chromos,' he insisted. 'I've been there before, and I know I am.'

'No, my friend,' Ori laughed, wagging her feathered tail. 'You must make yourself brave! We must find Cath and get into the aether, so that we can restore Tom's haunted soul to a place of rest. You know we must. It is the only thing to do.'

The last of the light was disappearing, and the cold night clenched about them. Another night outside, finding a hedge to shelter under. It didn't bother Danny; when he'd been travelling to the sea with Cath, they'd done plenty of this.

He felt a flash of courage. Loads of people would be scared, outside on a winter's night. He had Ori and Shimny, and he knew he'd be fine.

'OK then, how?' he asked, feeling Shimny's fur grow clammy in the evening dew. She would soon be recovered, and on her feet again. 'The only way to get to Chromos is to call the guardian, Zadoc, and he's gone. So who else is going to take us there? You?'

'I rather think,' said Ori, pushing her head underneath Shimny's body and closing her eyes, 'that we might have some other ideas in a minute.'

Through the edge of darkness the figure came up the lane towards them, and although there was hardly any of the twilight left to pick out her features, Danny could see that her hair was silver-grey and her eyes were red. The air that came with her was full of forgiving warmth and she walked with the steady tread of a person with a job that cannot be rushed.

What was Death doing here? Nobody had died.

Then Danny realised with a terrible stab of pain that no matter how hard he pushed his hand into Shimny's skin, he could feel no heat from it at all. What he had thought to be calm, shallow breathing had been nothing more than the breeze picking at her patched old coat.

He couldn't bear it. Was every creature around him to die? First Tom, now the gallant Shimny – everything he touched seemed to shrivel with the poison from his fingertips. The horse's head in his lap was as heavy as a slab of stone. She had run for his life, and she had died for him.

No tears came to him. His sorrow was the blade of an axe, twisting itself around inside his chest until it was raw and bleeding and begging for peace. And it was a peace that could never come now. Shimny was older than his entire world; for all he knew, she might be older than the land itself, and he had taken her from it, and knelt with her head on his lap as the last stream of life flowed from her.

He wanted to leap up and push Death away, but the old woman came to stand before him, and her red eyes defied him to touch her.

'We meet too often, you and I,' said Death, smiling gently. 'I'm sorry for it.'

Danny tried to breathe, tried to find his voice. 'Please don't take her.'

'But she's gone already. I'm just collecting what is owed to the earth. It's not a sad thing – I will return her sand to peace, back into the cycle of the world. That is my one task, and I do it. Always.'

'I need her,' said Danny.

Death shook her head. 'You have all you need. You have a bright, shining heart. You have courage. You even have a dog, now, it seems. You cannot claim this horse as well. She deserves better.'

And Danny knew she was right. It wasn't his place to ask for Shimny's life. She had belonged to herself, and she alone was setting off with Death. He couldn't hold her back to make himself feel less guilty.

He choked, unable to breathe past the spines in his throat. Muddled thoughts came flooding into his head: the great plain of Chromos, Shimny flying across it, the solid earthiness of her. She should return to the earth, like all other normal creatures. It was what he wanted for himself, for Tom and even Ori, one day. They should all go back to the earth they had come from, and stay a part of it, to be eaten by worms and sung ballads about.

But Shimny had given him wings. And he knew suddenly what he had to do.

When he was on Shimny's back, the world shone for him, whichever world he was in. If he could get into Chromos on Shimny, he'd feel as brave as a lion in there.

'She had a mighty heart,' he said. 'She was brave and fast and her heart was the biggest. She didn't think she was special. But she does deserve better, you're right. She should be Guardian of Chromos.'

Death raised an eyebrow, sharp even through the darkness.

'I have nothing to do with Chromos,' she said.

'But maybe you know how it works? Zadoc's gone, and Chromos needs a Guardian.'

'Chromos is Sammael's business. Are you trying to play his game now?'

Danny shook his head. 'Never. But I did something wrong – I left someone behind, somewhere, and now they're in torment; they're pulling shadows over the world – you must have seen the shadows. I have to get back to Chromos – there's only one person I know who might be able to help me put things right, and Chromos is the only way I can get to her.'

Death was silent for a moment, and then she said, very quietly, 'I wonder what I did to you, when I fed you The Book of Storms. I wonder what Sammael has done to you.

But perhaps the question you should ask is: what are you doing to yourself?'

'I'm trying to win,' said Danny. 'It's really hard.'

Death threw back her head and laughed to the sky, and the stars trembled. Then she knelt down on the other side of Danny, sinking slowly to the ground as if her back was stiff and causing her pain. She put a hand on Shimny's cold neck.

'And you think I should help you win, is that right?' she said, looking Danny squarely in the face.

Her red eyes burned into his own, very tired ones. It hurt to hold her gaze, but he held it.

'Yes,' he said. 'I only want what's right.'

'Careful,' said Death. 'I am no judge of rights and wrongs. My interest lies in seeing that the world is tidied up according to my own standards.'

And Death considered, until the road was so dark that Danny began to worry about passing cars, although none had come along in the hour or so they'd been there. Then he began to worry about the shadows. What if they came over in darkness, too? There'd be no way to tell except by listening out for the silence.

An owl hooted in the distance. He strained to hear more.

Ori cuddled against him and he listened to her breathing. Her steady patience was as comforting as her warmth.

Then Death took her hands away from Shimny's neck and looked at him shrewdly.

'I can't make this horse the Guardian of Chromos,' she said.

Danny's heart drained with despair.

'But I can leave her soul alone,' said Death. 'She will not be at peace. She will wander over the earth and through Chromos, looking for a place to lay her head. She will know nothing of the peace she deserves. It is the worst of fates. But lost souls may travel in the lowest part of Chromos, because they are immune to both fear and hope. They certainly can't fly in Chromos, or reach other worlds through it, if that's what you're hoping. But they can stumble along the floors of both worlds for eternity, grazing their knees against all the broken hopes that they'll never have. Is that what you want for this horse?'

Danny shook his head. 'When we've gone – when we've got there – couldn't you come and take her soul, then?' he asked.

'No,' said Death. 'I could not. If she is to be of use to you, I must forsake her entirely. If you wanted her to find peace, you would have to find a way to bestow it yourself.'

'But if you took her now?'

'If I took her now, she would return to the earth and be free.'

And I would have to find another way to get into Chromos, concluded Danny.

He let himself think once more, briefly, of what Shimny had done for him – how she had carried him on her back, saved his life twice, at least.

The horse's cold head lay heavy as an anchor in his lap. I'm sorry, he said. I'm going to do something awful to you. But when things are right with Tom, I'll put them right with you too. One day. I swear it, on my whole life.

He looked up at Death. Her red eyes were patient and kind. She looked, for a brief moment, like a harmless old woman, about to invite Danny into her home and offer him a biscuit from a rusty tin. But Danny wasn't fooled.

'Leave her,' he said, his voice breaking. 'Leave her behind. I'll get her back to you, one day.'

'You won't,' said Death. 'You'll have to find somewhere else for her. Once I forsake her, I cannot change my mind. Do you understand that?'

Danny nodded.

'Then I forsake her,' said Death. 'Death forsakes Shimny. Let her wander about the worlds until the end of time; I will have none of her. Her soul belongs nowhere. She came from the earth – she came from the stars and the galaxies. But she shall never return to them again. She is cast out.'

Danny bowed his head over the horse's body, half expecting it to come alive again in his hands, but it remained stiff and cold.

Death got up slowly, turned, and began to walk away.

'Wait!' croaked Danny. 'What do I do with her?'

'Nothing,' said Death. 'Go on your way. She'll find you. You'll be the first person she looks for.'

Shimny came in the hour before dawn, as Danny and Ori were huddled together in the shelter of a ruined stone shed, trying to keep warm. Even Ori's long coat was no protection against the wind's frozen teeth. Neither could sleep.

The dog leapt to her feet, lips drawn back from snarling fangs. She growled.

'What is it, Ori?' asked Danny. But he knew. He could feel it too.

The ghost came charging in, her eyes white with panic. She pawed at the ground, lunged at Danny, struck out at the dog, but her pale hooves could not cause them pain.

'What did you do to me?' she screamed, her eyes flashing gold. 'Where am I?'

Danny followed Ori's lead and backed away, letting Shimny lash out with hooves and teeth until she discovered that there was nothing here she could hit or bite.

At last she stood, head down, in the middle of the ruined hovel and her eyes faded again to white.

Dying hadn't been kind to her. Her once-black patches had faded to a mothy grey. Her ears were flat against her lumpy old head, and her back sagged even more deeply than the crescent moon shape it had taken on in her old age. Her lower lip trembled.

'I'm sorry,' said Danny.

'Tell me what you did,' said Shimny.

'I – well, Death – forsook you.'

Danny got to his feet and went towards the horse. He wanted to put out his hand and touch her neck, but when he tried to it felt like shrivelled snakeskin, and the horse flinched at his touch.

'Death? Why?'

'Because . . .' Because I asked her to, thought Danny. But he couldn't say it. 'Because it's the only way you can get into Chromos.'

'Chromos? What is Chromos?'

Danny was going to explain it to her, all about the land of colours and the way you could see your greatest dreams in it, and travel through it to anywhere. But he could see from the state of her that she had no hope left. It wouldn't be fair to make her think she'd see wonderful things in Chromos.

So he said, 'It's somewhere we need to go. Imagine what it might be like, and you can take us there.'

'I can't imagine anything,' wailed the horse. 'I'm lost.'

'Then you need to imagine the way home,' said Danny, feeling like a traitor as Shimny threw up her head, her eyes flashing gold again.

'Yes!' she said. 'Home! I must get home! It can't be far away!'

Danny jumped up onto her back and held out his arms to Ori, who was still rigid in the corner, hackles risen.

'Deal with it,' he said to her. 'If I have to do things I don't want to, so do you.'

And Ori, stiff-legged and suspicious, obeyed him. She came out from the corner and stepped towards the ghost, rigid with reluctance. When she was close enough, Danny reached down, grabbed her under her front legs, and lifted her onto Shimny's back. Ori was heavy, and it took a lot of scrambling, but finally she was perched on the broad shoulders in front of Danny, balancing with her paws wide apart.

Danny had a sudden feeling that things had fallen into place: he was on the back of a horse, about to leap up onto the great plain of Chromos. This time, he wasn't going home, leaving the colour and the dreams behind him. He and Ori were going in search of Cath. Very soon they would all set out for the furthest reaches of the world again. Tom's shadows weren't a disaster: they were a temporary problem. Together with Ori and Cath, Danny knew he could find a way to bring colour back to the flooded grey world.

'OK then,' he said, feeling his heart quicken with a nameless thrill. 'Go home, Shimny. Step up into Chromos, and fly there!'

Chapter 8

The House on the Beach

The air around them began to shake. If there was a magic in getting to Chromos, then Danny knew he had found it now – it had grown in his blood, and soaked him through. There was the great plain stretching out in front of him, vast and wide and green, with no fences or roads – a free expanse of world, waiting for the visions of those who journeyed through. Chromos was no longer a mysterious land of dreams: it was Danny's own country.

He imagined medieval knights and there they were, thundering past him on their chargers, coloured banners streaming. He imagined eagles and hawks and they flew above him, their wings cutting cleanly through the air. He imagined elephants and giraffes and they stalked along beside him, their eyes bright.

If only I could just bring the whole world up here, he thought. It would sparkle.

Ori had her eyes closed.

'You can look,' he said. 'Think of all the good things you want, and look!'

But the dog kept her eyes tightly shut. She leant back into him, pressing her fur against his chest, and he felt suddenly that all the positions of things had been reversed. In here, he was stronger than her.

He brought to mind a vision of Cath. He painted the picture of the little house beyond the sand dunes, the wide, windswept beach, and he felt it hovering in the distant air in front of him. There was a road that led there, and he was on that road, being drawn irresistibly along it.

But – wait! He was in Chromos! Why didn't he just bring Tom back to life in here? He could explain to him how sorry he was, how much he missed him, how he was going to try and make sure that everyone back home began to remember him . . .

At once, the sky in Chromos began to darken. And then the silence came.

He looked over his shoulder. Behind him, the great green plain of Chromos was turning grey, and the blue sky was turning grey. Nothing was safe from the shadows.

Danny pushed Shimny into a gallop. *Don't think about Tom. Don't think about Tom* – and the shadows gained on him, deadly and silent. He heard the silence falling and the colours dying, and grief pounded in his heart as strongly as the pounding of Shimny's hooves. These shadows were inside him; they were made of sorrow. He could not escape them by going to Chromos.

Shimny galloped over mountains so high she had to skate

over snowdrifts, and through rivers so deep that she had to swim, and the miles and miles passed by in a blur. The grass changed to rocks, the rocks to ice and snow and water, then back to rocks again, and finally to sand.

They galloped up a beach. It was a place that Danny had only seen once before, but he would never forget the bleakness of it – the white sands and stone-grey sea, and the dunes with their coarse grasses shivering in the wind.

'Go back to earth!' he shouted, tugging at Shimny's mane.

'But we're not home!' she shouted back. 'We're going home! It's up here, I know it is!'

'No, it's not!' said Danny, yanking at the mane and trying to shed the desire to be in Chromos from the inside of his mind.

'You said it was!'

'I lied!'

He tore a handful of Shimny's mane out, but it vanished in his hand and was back on her neck in an instant. Of course. She was a ghost.

'You lied?' The horse slowed for a moment, veering towards the choppy sea.

'Yeah,' said Danny. 'You can't get home through here. This is just where I needed to go. I needed you to bring me.'

His heart felt like a little lump of rotten bread – squashed and crumbling. It was worse than anything he had ever done, giving poor Shimny false hope.

Shimny came to an abrupt halt. 'My home isn't here?'

Her head hung low, the wind snatching at her mane. Danny hated himself.

He thought harder about falling through the air, dissolving the whole world around him, wrapping up the pieces of it and putting them away.

And it worked. Shimny's knees began to bend: she walked down a slope that Danny couldn't see, her hooves heavier with every step. Ori sat like a rock in Danny's arms.

He felt nothing of the triumph he had felt going into Chromos as they landed again, back on Earth. The victory seemed hollow, when he looked down at Shimny's neck.

Without looking around him, he kicked her on and they trudged up the beach towards the place where the dunes parted and the path began. In the dreary winter morning, the sand was a pale yellowy-grey, pitted with the prints of animals and birds.

When they reached the dunes, Ori jumped down from Shimny's back and shook herself out, golden fur flying. Then she put her muzzle up to the wind and sniffed, standing with one paw raised in the direction of the path.

Danny looked up. The path wasn't long, only a couple of hundred metres. A cold coastal sunshine drifted along most of it until it stopped at the front of a small garden, which sat around a low, whitewashed cottage.

Whitewash, Danny thought. That's new. Cath's tidied the place up. That's the most unlikely thing I've ever seen.

But the dog wasn't pointing at the whitewashed house. She was pointing at the sky behind, around and above it.

And the sky was filled with grey cloud.

'What do we do?' asked Danny.

'Go closer?' suggested Ori. 'See if there's a clear way in?'

Danny swung his leg over Shimny and jumped to the ground. 'We'll get shadowed,' he said. 'We'll go grey and lose all hope, same as back home.'

The shadow over the house looked old and settled, as though it had long since done its job, and afterwards fallen into a deep sleep. But Danny didn't believe that the shadows were weaker. They felt just as strong, and they called out to him to come closer, so they could smother him too. He didn't want to take a single step towards them.

'We have to go up to it,' said Ori. 'What other choice do we have? Come, just to the edge. The stick will help you a little, won't it?'

Danny left Shimny standing at the gap between the dunes, and kept a hand on Ori's warm fur as they walked up the sandy path together. That silence. How he hated it. Near the sea, the air should be full of hissing waves, calling birds and wind rustling through the grasses.

Here, there was nothing.

He tried not to look too hard at the shadow, but he couldn't avoid it once they reached the gate of the little garden: the shadow covered the house and stopped straight across the garden path, about a metre from the front door.

Danny stood for a second, then opened his mouth and cleared his throat.

'Cath?' he called. 'Cath, are you there?'

There was no answer from the house.

Danny opened the gate and took another step forward. 'Cath? Barshin?'

Again, nothing.

He looked around at the neat little garden. Someone had been growing vegetables: dark green leaves flourished in tidy rows. The front of the garden was still clear of shadow, bathing in the cold light. Behind him, Shimny stood, a distant figure on the beach, lost in misery.

Danny fought the rational voice in his head that told him nothing could have survived here. He turned back to the house and looked into the shadowy doorway.

The door was slightly ajar. If he could get something to push it with, he could stand just at the edge of the shadows and shove it open. It needn't even be very long – in fact, if he shuffled forward so that his toes were just touching the dark line of shadow – he could almost reach with his fingertips –

Pushing his arm into the shadowed doorway was like plunging it into an icy sea. Perhaps the shadows cooled down as they sat still. Perhaps if he went home now, he'd find it frozen into icebergs, grey and gleaming.

No, Danny thought. Ice looks alive. This cold isn't due to temperature – I bet if I stuck a thermometer under it, it would read just the same as out here. This cold is due to lack of colour.

And what that meant, he understood more and more each time he looked into the shadows. The colours were hot and tiring, they demanded you keep thinking, keep fighting. The grey asked nothing of you, and gave you nothing in return.

There was a strong pull in the grey, but once it had sucked you in, you were lost.

His fingers began to feel heavy, and he pulled his arm out of the shadows.

Ori was looking up at him. 'What are you waiting for?'

Danny glared at her.

'I'm not mocking you,' said Ori. 'I just think you could be a bit more impulsive. You've got that bit of stick, haven't you? Push open the door with it.'

'Yes, thanks,' said Danny. 'I had thought of that.'

He shoved the taro forward. This time, his hand and arm didn't feel cold. The stick stayed tight in his fingers as he poked the door open.

It swung inwards. Danny peered into the gloom. The interior of the house, snug and small, was too dark to make out. He opened his eyes as wide as possible, but it was no use, he was still standing in the light. If he wanted to see in the dark, he would have to be in the dark.

'Cath?' he tried again. 'Cath? Barshin? Are you there? It's me, Danny.'

He thought he heard a slight sound inside the house – a shuffling, or a scraping.

The stick felt solid in his hand. He had never truly known the extent of its power – it let him talk to every creature on earth, and it protected him from being killed by storms. But could it really help keep his heart alive if he stepped into the shadows?

'Can you hear anything?' he asked Ori, who was hanging back at his heels.

'Yes,' said Ori. 'There's something moving in there. But you shouldn't go in.'

'I thought you told me to?'

'I've changed my mind. Don't risk it. It could be just a rat, and if you were pulled in by the shadows, you'd be grey for nothing.'

She was shuffling backwards, shrinking away.

Danny frowned. 'What about being brave?'

'The shadows are . . . colder than I thought they'd be,' said Ori. 'I don't want you to come to any harm.'

'Well, neither do I,' said Danny. 'But I reckon I'm going to have to risk it. Unless you can smell what's in there?'

Ori sniffed at the air. 'I smell the sea, and a hundred scents of green leaves and grasses and sand. A very complex map, actually . . . Some kind of fox has been around here, and an old lady who washes in water from deep underground, not salty water, and her clothes are hung about with the scents of hedgehog poo and mouse wee, and she herself wees on the vegetables in the garden . . .'

'I don't really need to know about that,' said Danny hastily. 'It would be more helpful if you could smell anything inside the house.'

'No I can't,' said Ori. 'It is as scentless as – as – as scentless as if somebody had kicked me on the back of my head and turned my nose off. Which did happen to a dog I knew once, when I was a puppy.'

As if someone had turned your nose off.

Danny stared into the dark room. That was it – under the shadows, it was as though someone had kicked you on the head and turned down all your senses. You forgot you were a living, hearing, smelling, dreaming human, with the power to imagine up worlds inside your own head, and you saw only grey.

He thought of the strong colours of Chromos. If he could hold Chromos in his head, surely that, together with the stick, would give him enough protection to run quickly in and out of the shadows. If only he'd been able to bring a fragment of Chromos down to earth with him.

But Chromos was only half real. It was a land of imagination – and he still had his own imagination, here. If he picked a few things on earth that had colour, and memorised them, maybe that would do just as well.

He did not let himself look back at Shimny or the beach, or the white sky. Instead, he took a long glance at the garden and counted five things in it – a twisted brown tree, the green leafy plants, a thorny yellow bush, a tuft of pale blue-grey sea-grasses, and a black bird sitting on a fence.

Five alive, colourful things. Brown tree. Green plants. Yellow bush. Blue grass. Black bird.

'OK, then,' he said. 'Wish me luck.'

And then he stepped forward into the doorway of the house, and into the shadow.

Chapter 9

Inside

It was cold, but the heat from the stick kept flowing down Danny's arm, warming his shoulder. He felt it reaching his heart, just about. That was the key.

Danny walked into the house and let his eyes adjust to the darkness. In seconds his feet became heavier, as though the floor was trying to cling to the soles of his trainers.

The room was sparsely furnished, and every piece of furniture was made of chunks of wood. Driftwood, Danny guessed, although there was no smell of the sea to confirm it. There was no smell of anything at all, only a damp, dark prickling at the back of his neck that told him not to linger here.

He felt the shadows pressing down at the prickles. *Why fight us? We are easy to live with. Just forget the colour. Give in to us. Stay.*

Brown tree. Green plants. Yellow bush. Blue grasses. Black bird. Danny chanted the words under his breath, and each word reminded him of the colours outside, the warmth of the stick in his hand.

But the warmth was struggling to reach his heart now. He cast his eyes around quickly for Cath, or any sign of a living creature.

She was lying in a corner, clutching a bundle of rags. Her head was slumped against another lump of driftwood, and her body was sprawled, as though she'd tripped over something and not bothered to move. She was completely still.

Danny took three steps towards her. She didn't seem to hear him, or know he was there.

He didn't think twice before grabbing her, expecting her to strike out at him, to push him away. But she did nothing at all when he yanked her arm. Her body hung like a rag doll from his grip, and she wasn't heavy, but all of her weight was dead.

In the end it was easier for Danny with his one spare hand to pull her out leg-first. He dragged her through the doorway, into the little garden and out of the shadows.

His heart threw itself about his chest, as panicked as a bird in a chimney. The stark daylight forced him to close his eyes, and he sank to his knees.

Ori stood over Cath sniffing uncertainly at her.

'She's alive,' the dog said. 'I think.'

'Of course she's alive,' snapped Danny, opening his eyes again. 'Nothing could kill Cath.'

But as he looked at her, he was afraid for a second that his heart might fly into his mouth and escape through his teeth.

Cath was grey. Her skin was grey. Her once-black hair was

grey. The clothes she wore, the bundle of rags she clutched, the tattered shoes on her feet – they were all grey.

He checked himself. The football kit was still dark red. The five coloured things had worked for him.

Brown tree. Green plants. Yellow bush. Blue grasses. Black bird.

The words rattling around his head came to him again as he knelt over Cath's body. She lay unmoving, the sea breeze playing with her grey hair, and the sea grasses scratching at her grey skin.

The colours of the five things had all jumped out at him. What if he brought them to her? Might they banish her greyness, too?

A piece of the brown tree did nothing. Leaves from the dark green plants lay for a moment on her chest before the wind picked them up and whisked them away. Danny had pretty much lost hope by the time he got to snapping off a bit of the bush – Cath was already lying in the blue-grey grass, and he doubted he would be able to persuade a bird to jump onto her grey body.

'What are you?' he asked the bush, before he took a piece. 'Have you got any magical powers?'

'None that I know of,' said the bush. 'I am a gorse bush. When I flower, I smell – so they say – of coconuts. I personally think coconuts may well smell of gorse, but I have never met one, so I can't be entirely sure.'

'Can I break a bit off you?' asked Danny.

'By all means,' said the gorse bush. 'I'm hard as nails. You won't hurt me.'

Danny took a piece of spiky twig to Cath, and lifted her hand off the bundle of rags. He curled her fingers around the spines. Even if she hurt herself on the thorns, it could be a good thing just to feel pain.

Nothing happened. He turned away to see if he could spot a bird to talk to.

'Danny!'

Ori's voice barked out behind him, hot and excited.

Danny turned. Cath's hair had begun to darken, creeping back towards the ebony black of a midnight sky. Her skin was warming; her clothes and the bundle of rags were taking on shades of colour.

His eyes went to the gorse twig in her hand.

The back of her hand was covered in yellow flowers. They grew up her skin, over her wrist, and halfway up her arm.

Now he remembered – he'd seen them on her hand before. He'd asked her what they were, a lifetime ago in the farmhouse kitchen, and she told him they were flowers she'd touched in Chromos – yellow flowers she liked, and they'd grown up her hand, dyeing her skin with a tattoo of twining plants.

Without even thinking about it, he must have had that in the back of his mind when he'd chosen the gorse as one of his five colours to remember. And the flowers had blown on a glowing ember inside Cath, raising flames strong enough to reawaken her colour.

Cath lay on the grass, her eyes closed. Then her lips moved, and a single word came out. Danny didn't even have to hear it to know what it would be.

'Barshin,' Cath said.

Cath and the hare were inseparable. Without bothering to protest, Danny readjusted his grip on the stick, turned his back on Ori, Cath, and the free, open world, and ducked back into the shadows again.

He was colder from the start, this time. And Barshin was much harder to spot – a limp bundle of fur and bones, huddled in a corner.

Danny felt a stab of dark hatred as he took hold of the hare's hind leg and lifted it up. The surge was strong enough to stop his breath and make his chest hurt.

He saw it again, in a flash of cruel brightness.

Tom's death.

A blaze of flame, climbing up towards the sky, and Tom falling down the wind into the fire, being eaten up by the flames.

Barshin the hare had betrayed them all, and Tom's soul had fallen into Sammael's hands, and Sammael had killed him.

Danny gripped the hare's leg, dangling the creature in the air. Barshin hung helpless before him.

He could decide whether the hare lived or died.

His hand went limp, as though preparing to drop the hare onto the beaten earth floor. He could just go outside, carry Cath away, and say that he hadn't been able to find Barshin, that the hare must already have shrivelled to nothing under the shadows.

Danny clenched his fingers around the hare's leg, feeling fury rise up inside him. He used the sudden flush of heat to turn and run from the house, and this time he pulled the door shut behind him, and as he stepped into the daylight, he threw Barshin down on the path and vowed that he was not going back inside the shadows again, not now, not ever.

'What happened?' Danny asked. 'When did you get shadowed?'

Cath was sitting up on the grass, looking around her. She wasn't quite human-coloured yet, but she wasn't entirely grey any more. Cradling Barshin in her arms, she was trying to bring warmth back into his grey fur by pressing as much of herself as she could to his long body. For a second, Danny thought she was about to bury her face in the hare's stomach.

Instead, she looked up at him. Her eyes were as dark as he'd always known them, shining strongly with scorn.

'Why did you come?' she asked, quietly.

'I had to come and get you,' said Danny. 'The shadows came over – I thought they were Sammael, but before that I nearly drowned, and I saw Tom –'

He waited for her face to register blankness, for her to ask him who Tom was. But she was Cath, and she knew everything. Of course she knew about Tom.

'You've remembered him?' she asked. 'How?'

'I saw him under the sea. But everyone else has forgotten him. How did you remember?'

'Barshin,' she said simply. 'Barshin kept telling me the story of what we did, how I ended up where I was. I didn't remember it, but he told me it was true, so I still knew it.'

Barshin stirred in Cath's arms. His fur was losing its greyness, returning to a mid sandy-brown. Danny looked at Cath, her eyes haunted and sunk, her hair wild. She had her back turned to the cottage and she wasn't trying to see what had happened to it.

'Well,' he said, trying to be brisk and sound brave, 'I think Tom's bringing the shadows over. We've got to find him again, and stop him.'

Barshin stopped struggling and Cath set him down onto the ground. The hare crouched in the tufted grass, flicking his ears. 'Somebody has the book,' he muttered.

Danny ignored him. The hare might be Cath's friend, but Danny had nothing to say to Barshin, and he was sure that the hare had nothing to say that he wanted to hear. He explained his idea about Tom caught in the aether, cast into hopeless torment, and how it fitted very well with the shadows.

Cath thought, then shrugged. 'I guess it could be like that.'

'It is,' said Danny. 'I'm sure of it.'

Cath stared at him and opened her mouth, and for a second he knew she was about to contradict him, to tell him that he'd got it wrong. But the moment passed, and suddenly she didn't seem to have the energy to argue.

'So we should try and get to the aether, then? But there's no Zadoc any more. We can't even get into Chromos.'

'We can get to Chromos,' said Danny. He explained about Shimny. 'She can't go higher up in there, though. She has to stay on the floor. Would you know how to imagine another way in?'

86

'Well, yeah, we got to the aether through the moonlight on the sea, once, didn't we?' said Cath. 'I guess we could try to see that on the floor of Chromos, if we want to.'

'Of course!' Danny scrambled to his feet. Why hadn't he thought of that himself? It was so simple.

Because Cath was the one who thought about what might be possible before she told herself it was impossible, that was why.

Danny held his hand out to Cath. 'Come on, let's do it.'

'Sure.' She took his hand and got up, still clutching her bundle of coloured rags, and they went back down the path to Shimny, with Ori and Barshin bounding ahead.

Shimny was standing in the same spot, head lowered. When they reached the horse, Cath put a hand out to touch her.

'How long can she stay in Chromos?' Cath asked.

Danny shrugged. 'Dunno. Forever, I guess. Until I find her a home.'

Cath's lips tightened thoughtfully, then she said, 'If I say I'll find her a home, can I have her? After we've found Tom, I mean.'

'Why?' Danny frowned. 'You've got all this. The house and everything. It'll be fine again once the shadows go.'

Cath shook her head. 'It was,' she said. 'Ida – the old woman who lived here – she sold her soul to Sammael so she could live in the wild and never have to see no one she didn't want to see, and I thought that's what I wanted, too. Ida didn't mind me staying; she knew I was like her, and I was happy for a bit. But then all the nightmares came, about Dad and the flat and

Johnny White – you know, that guy he done away with – and when I woke up every morning, the walls were closer and closer, and I'd run outside and look at the mountains, and they'd get closer and closer, and all I could think about was running up them and over them and never stopping again.'

Danny looked into her tough face, hating the despair on it. Cath was always confident. The grey inside her was making her betray herself.

'But . . . that's just the shadows,' he said. 'This house was the best dream you ever had. When the shadows have gone, you'll want it again.'

Cath shook her head. 'It ain't the shadows – it happened way before they came. It's me. I don't want a home. I don't need one. I just need to keep on looking for one. I need to be in Chromos, where I can always imagine up new places to go – as long as I can always go there, I'll be happy. Maybe not even happy. Just – alive.'

'But you can't live in Chromos. Chromos isn't . . .'

Chromos wasn't what? Danny broke off. He had been about to say 'Chromos isn't real', but he knew that Cath would tell him he was talking rubbish. She believed it was a complete new world. 'OK then,' he said instead. 'When we've done, I'll let Shimny go with you. But you'll have to find her a home in the end. I promised her.'

He scrambled up onto Shimny. The sea had taken on a steely grey sheen, and the white crests of waves were dancing a little more wickedly in the picked-up breeze.

'It'll storm,' said Cath. 'It always does when it starts looking like that.'

'Will you go back into Chromos?' Danny asked Shimny. 'We need to get back there.'

'But it's not my home, is it?' said Shimny, without hope in her voice. 'You won't help me find my home. I'll always be wandering about, friendless and alone . . .'

Danny found that he wanted to snap at her that home really wasn't all it was cracked up to be, especially when the people who were supposed to look after you there decided to leave, or a galloping shadow ate it up and turned it into a grey pit, but he'd been mean enough already to Shimny.

If only everyone could just be happy again.

So he said, 'After we've sorted things out, Cath will help you find your home. She promises she will. And she never breaks a promise.'

Shimny raised her head and said, 'Really?'

'Really,' Danny assured her.

'I'll go, then!' said Shimny, her mane rippling in the breeze. 'I like the look of that girl – she's got a wild heart! I'll go now! Chromos, is it? I'll go!'

It was a tight scramble but they all made it, somehow, with Cath behind Danny, Ori in front of him and Barshin nestled in the rags in Cath's arms. It was a good job Shimny's back was so dipped – at least it anchored them in.

'To Chromos!' Danny said, and Shimny launched herself forwards.

The world began to dissolve, as before. Danny waited for the colours to grow strong and the great plain to open up before them. He expanded his heart to it, held the best of his dreams in his mind. One day he'd write an entire graphic novel, full of weird and wonderful beasts that explained the world in legends and stories, and he would pour every bit of Chromos that he'd ever seen into it, so that everyone who read it would be touched by colour.

But the world began to go grey.

At first Danny didn't believe it. OK, it had been shadowed before, but that had been when he'd let grief about Tom shadow his heart, and he wasn't thinking with sadness about Tom now, because he was going to get Tom back; he was going to solve everything.

But Chromos was a thick, grey shadow, and nothing else.

Danny's shoulders froze, then his chest, then his legs, until the only warmth came from the stick in his pocket, a single tiny line of heat pressing against his thigh.

He began to shiver.

It was Cath's fault. And Barshin's. They were infected with the shadows.

'Get off!' he screamed at Cath. 'You brought the shadows! You're making it grey!'

'No!' shouted Cath, as the world rocked and buffeted them about. 'It's not me, it's you! You see what's in *your* head, here!'

Danny began to choke: his lungs couldn't draw in enough air. He couldn't see, either – Chromos was a shuttered room, where the thin light that seeped in through the cracks served only to cast more shadows. Ahead of them, the shadows thickened. They couldn't push through, or break out.

They had to go back to Earth.

'Go back to the beach!' he yelled at Shimny, clutching Ori's golden fur to his chest. 'We're dying!'

'But you said you had to come here,' squealed Shimny. 'I've got to go through here to help you, and then the girl will find my home.'

'Go back!' Danny screamed. 'You'll kill us all!'

He fought her with all that he could – the will to fall from Chromos, to land back on the wide, brown beach, to sail over the choppy waves. He pulled at everything he could see in his mind: the sea-grasses, the sand, the twisted trees – until at last they were tumbling back down onto the earth.

Chapter 10

The Book of Shadows

They landed in a mess of clinging arms and flailing legs, Shimny nose-down in the sand. Danny, Cath, dog and hare slid off, tangling together on the beach.

'You spoilt it!' Danny sat up, spitting out sand. 'You took the shadows with you! Into Chromos!'

Cath pushed him back down again as she sat up. 'Idiot!' she said scornfully. 'You see what *you* see in there. Have you forgotten even that? If it's grey for you up there, then that's because you've let the grey inside you. I told you so.'

It hit him around the face like a sudden gust full of sea spray, and although he said, once, she doesn't know anything, she's not the old Cath, he saw that she was right. While he'd been saving Barshin, he'd remembered too vividly what had happened to Tom. He couldn't stop watching the flames, over and over, in his own head. He had cast a shadow over his own heart, and Chromos was closed to him.

He looked out to sea angrily, and chucked handfuls of sand down the beach.

'Don't despair,' said Ori, shuffling closer to him. 'There's always a way. You're brave and strong and persistent. You'll find it.'

Danny shook his head and narrowed his eyes as Barshin hopped a couple of paces down the beach, coming into Danny's line of sight. For a second Danny almost saw the shape of the stag, Isbjin al-Orr, galloping up the beach towards them. Stag and hare – there had been something about the two of them that cast an air of enchantment on that journey they had all made, as though it might slip, one day, into legend, and be told to the children of stags and the children of hares for all time.

There's nothing legendary about *this* journey, thought Danny, grinding a savage fist into the sand. It isn't going anywhere.

Barshin turned and looked at Danny, and said, 'Are you ready to hear what I've got to say yet?'

'I shouldn't think so,' snapped Danny. 'Given that it's probably a pack of lies, like last time.'

'You still think I have links with Sammael, then?'

'Don't you? He owns your soul, doesn't he?'

Barshin looked out to sea. 'That's true. I can't deny it. But I have carried out his task for him. I don't work for him any more.'

'And you reckon I'll believe that?' said Danny. 'Think again.'

'Listen,' said Barshin, his ears twitching in the nagging breeze. 'The shadows have affected us all. We can't free ourselves from them. They sit inside us, feeding and growing.

I was out hunting, and when I came back, I did not know what the grey was, and I ran straight into it. But Cath and the old lady, they were already gone.'

'What happened to the old lady?'

'When the shadows came, she wandered outside the house and fell in the garden. She hit her head on a stone and died. I think it was a merciful way to die. Cath was just lying and waiting for life to disappear.'

Danny winced. Barshin's tone was level and calm, but a little too matter-of-fact.

The hare continued. 'So we all lay down to die, one way or another. Cath was right – it was not our fault you could not travel in Chromos, and then easily find Tom. But nor could I, and nor could she. The truth is that now we are all shadowed.'

'Then I'll never get into the aether, will I? Unless we try waiting for a full moon and going in through the real sea, down here.'

'You said yourself, we have no time to wait for the full moon,' said Barshin. 'No – I spoke to you of something, and you did not want to hear. But I should tell you of it now.'

'Yeah? What's that? Another place I really ought to go to save Tom?' Danny laughed bitterly. 'I think I've heard that one before, correct me if I'm wrong.'

'Not a place,' replied Barshin calmly. 'There is a book.'

'Of course,' said Danny. 'A book I need to find. That sounds quite familiar, too, now you come to mention it.'

'Not to find,' said Barshin. 'You need to make it. I thought at first that the shadows must come from a creature who had discovered how to make this book. But now you say that you think the shadows are coming from Tom's trapped soul. If indeed that is the case, then I doubt Tom's soul has made this book. He would surely be doing much worse things with it, if he had. It is a very powerful book.'

'What could be worse than this?'

'Ah, I forgot how little imagination you have,' said Barshin, though his tone was practical and without judgement.

'Oh, shut up,' said Danny. 'Just tell me about this book. What's it called?'

'Well, you know the answer to that,' said Barshin. 'It's in your mind already. Turn it over and read the cover.'

'Don't be dumb,' snapped Danny. 'Just tell me.'

Barshin looked back towards the little house, and sniffed at the vein of nothingness that the wind carried past his nostrils.

'*The Book of Shadows*,' he said. 'Not hard to guess, was it?'

'It's witch stuff,' said Cath. 'Just a load of spooky old witch stuff. Ida was always banging on about it.'

'She knew of *a* book of shadows, to be sure,' said Barshin. 'There are many people who use the term to describe some book or other that they think has special powers. But I am not talking about your silly human affairs. *The Book of Shadows* is the book at the heart of all worlds.'

'Go on,' said Danny, despite himself.

Barshin nodded, and settled into a seated position on the sand.

'It is the first and earliest of the Dark Legends. These are not the stories we tell our young leverets – they would only serve to frighten. But at times, in places, as we grow older, we come to learn of them. Many hares know this story, though they rarely talk about it amongst themselves.

'We hares are not like you humans: always fighting to tell the big story, to prove that their own way is best. We bother only with stories that we know to be roughly correct. This may have been passed down through thousands of generations, but it is the true story of the real *Book of Shadows*. So put all others from your mind.

'In the beginning, there were two worlds. Each was owned by a hare – or, if that doesn't fit with your idea of who is important, you may make them people. It doesn't matter. What matters is that two worlds were made, almost identical, and the two creatures who made them, Mab and Xur –'

'Xur was an ox,' said Danny. 'I've heard about him.'

'Make them oxen, if you like,' said Barshin, without hesitating. 'Just pay attention. The two creatures, Mab and Xur, were both very proud of the worlds they'd made, and very displeased when they saw that they had competition. But while Mab was content to shrug her oxen-shoulders and say that she was sure they'd find room in the universe for both their earths, Xur was not so easily satisfied.

'For Xur saw that Mab had made a better world than he. To most creatures, as I said, these worlds seemed identical. But Xur's world had rules. It had boundaries. Structure. Limits. Some things were possible, and some were not. However, in Mab's world, any creature could do anything. Nothing was impossible. They only had to imagine it, and it would happen. If both worlds were to go on existing side-by-side, then very soon, Xur knew, they would look quite different. He was sure – almost entirely sure – that he had done a much better job, and that his world would be more stable, calmer, and more sweetly beautiful. But he rather suspected that Mab's world would be full of tempests and glory and free imagination.

'Jealous Xur decided to destroy Mab's world. He couldn't obliterate it completely – she was as powerful a creature as he – so he vowed to parcel it up and bury it, as a squirrel does with a nut in autumn. He sent Mab off on a fool's errand to collect the night, then took the four basic elements of his own world – earth, air, fire and water – and wrapped them around Mab's world. Clenching the wrapped bundle between his paws – or hooves – he squashed it into a tiny ball, turned it inside-out, wrapped it again, and when it was smaller than a pinhead, he tucked it carefully away in a shadow, and it was gone.

And when she returned, try as she might, Mab could not find it again. Too broken-hearted to build another new world, Mab slunk away into the misplaced night, and lives there to this day. Her world is lost. We must all live in the world of Xur, where some things are possible and some are not, until the end of days.

But Mab's world still exists, tucked away in that shadow. One day, so the legend foretells, the stories of the four elements – earth, air, fire and water – will be collected together and written down in a book. *The Book of Shadows* will be its name, and if it is taken back to the place where

Xur hid Mab's world, Mab's world will spring out of the shadow and unfurl from its wrappings. And the owner of the book will have such power as the world has never known – the power to transcend the possible, to reach into the impossible and paint its bright colours over the drab world of Xur. They will have the power to write the world anew, according to Mab's intention, and their own desires. And Xur's world will be forever changed.'

Danny looked out to the sea. The waves were swelling up, green-grey in the fading afternoon light. No ships on the horizon, no land or islands, only the endless cold shimmer of the sea, and the freewheeling birds.

Anything possible. Anything. To be able to do it, just like that – fix the world.

The shadows would go.

Sammael would die.

Shimny would find peace.

Cath would be free to live however she wanted.

Danny's parents would be happy and hopeful.

Paul would move to another school.

Aunt Kathleen would remember Tom.

Danny would live at home with Ori, until he grew up.

And one morning, Isbjin al-Orr the stag would come stepping into the garden, leaving clipped prints in the morning dew, and wait, head high, nostrils touching at the wind, for Danny to see him.

Danny would go downstairs, open the back door and step out into the quiet early morning, and feel the ice of the ground as he padded across it in bare feet. The soles of his feet would sting.

He would go up to the stag and put his hand on Isbjin al-Orr's neck, and feel the warmth under the wiry old coat.

The stag would dip his head.

Danny would get on his back.

Together, they would take off.

Into the fields.

Into the hills.

Into the wild, wild sea.

Danny's heart was seized by the memory of feeling strong and powerful and unafraid. He had been somebody else then, another person inside his own body. Perhaps he had been the stag, for a few long seconds, without fear of anything. Perhaps he had been neither human nor animal, but a third creature, immortal.

He shrank from the thought. The only creature he knew who was not recognisably of the earth was Sammael, and Danny had no desire to be like him.

But he wouldn't be like Sammael, no matter how much power he had.

He would be good.

'I can make the book,' Danny said to Barshin. 'I can talk to everything. I'll get the stories of the four elements and make the book, and put everything back to how it should be.'

Barshin looked at him steadily. There was a yellow light in the hare's eyes, a touch of mad intensity that Danny hadn't seen before.

'You trust me, then?' Barshin said. 'I only have to offer you power, and you trust me?'

'I'll find out soon enough if you're lying,' said Danny.

'And what if you make *The Book of Shadows*, and Sammael gets hold of it? What if I've got you to make it just for him?'

'If I make it,' said Danny, 'the first thing I'll do is kill Sammael. Before anything else.'

'Before rescuing Tom?'

Danny scrambled to his feet. 'No! Yes! Before rescuing Tom. Or maybe I'll rescue Tom first and stop the shadows . . . but once Sammael's gone, I'll put the whole world to rights. I'll make it so that no one ever has to be afraid again. I'll make everything open – and clear.'

'Sounds daft to me,' said Cath.

Danny knew it wasn't daft – the more you discovered about the world, the more you came to understand how much of it was hidden, unwilling to explain itself. But sometimes – just sometimes – a crack appeared through the darkness, and some light shone through.

Ori came waddling to his side, plumy tale blowing in the sharpening wind.

'You're feeling happier,' she said, pushing her jowls against his leg.

'Yes,' he agreed. 'There's a plan. I just need to make a book . . .'

Danny found his hand, unbidden, curling itself around Ori's soft ear. It felt as delicate as a dried leaf. He resisted the urge to draw her closely to him and bury his face in her fur.

'Earth, air, fire and water,' he muttered. 'Well, that's easy. I talked to water before. I listened to air. I even touched fire, though I didn't hear it speak. I'll just ask them, one by one, and then I'll have everything I need.'

Chapter 11

The Elements

Danny tried the air first. He put his face up to the breeze and drew in a lungful. Cold, wet and sharp, it brought salt and sand and the clear call of the gulls down into his chest.

'Air?' he asked, but no answer came.

He pushed his thoughts up to the whole wide sky above the beach, above the sea. All of it – that vast space, bigger than everything else in the world put together.

'Air?' he tried. 'Air, can I ask you about *The Book of Shadows*?'

The air was silent. He listened hard to the things inside it, the gulls and sandflies and leaping crickets, and each had its voice. But the air told him nothing.

'What you up to?' asked Cath. Her voice was flat and tired, and when Danny glanced at her, she looked grey again. Not as bad as before, but definitely tinged around the edges.

'I'm trying to talk to the air,' he said. He didn't need to

explain anything more to Cath – he'd told her about the stick, long ago.

'Oh,' she said. She looked up at the sky and shuddered, and Danny saw that her hands were trembling.

'They won't get you again,' he said. He thought he should have added something like, I won't let them, I'll take care of you – but it seemed wrong, with Cath.

'They've already got me,' Cath said, shaking her head.

'No, I got you out. You're not under them any more. You're free, now. Human again.'

But she tightened her mouth, and her fists, and when she turned her eyes on him, the old fire in them was choked with smoke.

'They're in me,' she said. 'Right inside. You still won't ever believe what's actually there, if you don't like it. That's your problem. Why don't you try listening for once? Maybe that'll help you understand how to talk to things.'

For a second, he was tempted to argue back. But she was trying to help him, he supposed. In a sort of way.

He listened, even harder, to the whine of the wind and the shiver of the sea foam. There was something in the wind, for sure – a low, muttered chant, rising and falling and lifting at times to a wail, a warped echo of the skylarks that haunted the fields of Tom's farm.

Danny pulled the sound towards him, curling the fingers of his mind tightly around the wind's song.

'*Whenever the moon and stars are set*
Whenever the wind is high

103

All night long in the dark and wet
A man goes galloping –

Trotting . . . Scuttling . . . Oh blow! A man goes issuing . . .
No, that's not it – damn me, why did I turn the pages of
that book? And then she shut it! Damn girl . . . A man goes
echoing . . . Teetering . . . What does he do?'

'Riding?' suggested Danny. It was a poem he knew.

The wind swooped, plucked at his hair, scuttled under
Ori's tail, and gave poor Shimny a gust up her belly that
sent her into an even more miserable hunch.

'*Riding*!' it said, gleefully. 'Are you sure?'

'Yes,' said Danny. 'My dad used to read that to me, when I
was little. It's called "Windy Nights". It's about a highwayman.'

'Ooooh! I don't suppose you know the rest of it, do
you? I was playing with the girl's hair as she was reading
the book, and flicking the pages, and she got so irritated
that she closed the book and went into her house before
I'd finished reading the poem. Do you know how it ends?'

'Yeah,' said Danny. 'It goes:

Late in the night when the fires are out,
Why does he gallop and gallop about?
Whenever the trees are crying aloud,
And ships are tossed at sea,
By on the highway, low and loud,
By at the gallop goes he.
By at the gallop he goes, and then
By he comes back at the gallop again.'

104

He was very surprised that he'd remembered it; the poem brought back a strong glimpse, suddenly, of how he'd once been a small boy tucked up in bed, with his dad's low voice chanting in the light of the bedside lamp. Sometimes, after Dad had turned the light off and left the bedroom, Danny had listened to the wind outside the walls and imagined highwaymen outside on the dark roads, dodging the cars and lorries, looking for the ghosts of old coaches to rob.

The world of Mab, he thought. I knew it existed then.

And he was suddenly conscious of what a terrible betrayal he had committed in forgetting it, even for an instant.

A figure came into his mind – a tall, thin figure in a dark coat, hair curling around his bony skull, high boots up to his knees. Sammael.

If Danny had never met Sammael, he would still be back in his own house, all his childish imaginings forgotten. Sammael had brought him back to the world of Mab.

No, said Danny to himself, and pushed the vision away.

The wind was well pleased. It took the poem and swooped around the group on the beach, chanting and yelling out the words with great glee. Danny listened to it bellowing and singing, unable to stop himself smiling at the thought of highwaymen dodging around milk vans and cement lorries, leaping up and down kerbstones, pulling their horses to a halt at red traffic lights.

'Hey!' he called to the wind. 'Hey, I need a story from the air. Can you help me?'

'Ooooh, no,' said the wind, rattling his ears and pushing icy fingers down his neck. 'I'm not the air. I'm the wind!

Oooh, you've excited me so much, I'm going to go and whip the sea into a frenzy. We'll see what she thinks about highwaymen!'

'Wait!' said Danny. 'How can I talk to the air?'

'You can't!' shrieked the wind. 'No one can! Hee hee!'

Danny's heart dropped again, his hope forgotten. The wind was almost gone from him – he heard its voice louden, then fade, and the sea picked up angrily, harassed by the hectic gusts.

Ori said quietly, 'Don't despair. If it wasn't the answer you needed, let's keep asking.'

Danny stared out to sea for a second, watching the bristling path of the wind across the wave tops, then shrugged.

'OK,' he said. 'It's worth another go, I guess. Let's find some earth.'

Together with Ori, he set off back up the path that led towards the little house and garden. He tried not to look up at the house, but the rising wind forced his chin up as if showing it to him. Look what you've done, said the small voice of hate in his head.

I'm putting it right, he said to the voice. I'm doing everything I can.

Not enough, said the voice. You never do enough.

Danny pushed it away and stared hard at the ground.

In the end, he had to go all the way back to the little fenced garden before he found real soil. Kneeling, he pushed his fingers down into it, feeling the cold creep up his skin. Ori sat close to his side, watching him squash the damp earth.

Danny put his clean hand into the pocket of his trousers and took hold of the stick.

'Earth?' he said. 'Earth, can you hear me?'

The earth was silent. This was ridiculous. He knew the earth could speak, because he'd heard it before, when he'd fed it to a worm. The worms ate earth and sang songs of the life that the grains of earth had been. Only really, he thought now, that was the worms singing, not actually the earth.

This earth wasn't going to speak to him, even if it could.

'Don't despair,' said Ori. She pushed her wet nose against the muddy skin on the back of his hand. It was slimier than the mud, but he felt less alone at once.

He made his way back to Cath, Barshin and Shimny on the beach. 'It's no good,' he said. 'I don't think I can speak to the elements. Or they won't speak to me, I don't know which. I've tried air and earth – I guess fire might be worth a try . . .'

'Nah,' said Cath. 'If two of them won't, then maybe Barshin's story's just a bit wrong.'

Danny raised his eyebrows. 'I thought Barshin was always right?'

Cath grinned. 'Barshin is. But all them stories – they ain't all exact, are they? Anyway, I told you Ida was always on about witchy stuff, didn't I? Even she used to ramble on about *The Book of Shadows*. She was always saying that shadows were where things hid.'

'What sort of things?' Danny leant forward.

Cath shrugged. 'Stupid stuff.'

'About shadows? What was it? Try and remember! Anything!'

Cath shook her head. 'I didn't buy it. She thought you could trap shadows. There's a box on the windowsill in the kitchen she used to keep for putting 'em in. Honestly, it's rubbish. You can't put shadows in a box.'

Danny rolled his eyes. 'Where's the kitchen?' he said.

'Round the back.'

Round the back of the house.

Under the shadows.

Chapter 12

Four Friends

Danny made his way slowly down the path with Ori at his side, and stopped by the gate. He looked around him. The last rays of the sun had long since been blotted out by storm clouds. It was about to start raining; he could feel the wet edge to the air, and the bunching clouds above were dark and cold.

Nothing inside him wanted to go back into the house.

Perhaps he could go round to the back, and reach in through a window? He'd still be under the shadows, but not the double shadow of a cloud and a roof. And he'd have the small, temporary talismans – stick and colours.

'Wait here,' he said to Ori. 'I'll run around the back and see if I can break the window and grab the box.'

'Your heart,' said Ori. 'I fear for your heart. Don't do it.'

'I've got to, haven't I?' said Danny. 'I'll be fine.'

He pulled the stick from his pocket and looked at the house. No point in thinking further. He held the stick out, letting its warmth sweep up his arm, and ran forward.

To the house. Down the dark passage at the side, flanked by low bushes and trees. Around the back. The stretching garden, the vegetable plots, the stony paths.

The stony paths.

He caught a whiff of her before he saw her – a strong, sweet smell of rotten fruit and flies and old, rancid milk, concentrated in the still air. The smell dragged a wave of nausea into his stomach, wrapping it tightly into a knot.

The old woman. Ida. Lying on the ground, curled and white.

This was what the shadows brought. This.

Danny forced himself to pick up a stone, smashed a small window next to the back door and reached inside, feeling about on the windowsill. His fingers closed around something – rectangular, smooth sides, some kind of raised design on the top. The box, it had to be.

The coldness was creeping into his heart. No – the smell was creeping there, up from his stomach, invading his lungs and his blood. It was the smell of the end of the world.

Danny grabbed the box and pushed himself away from the window frame. His hand stung as he touched it – the world was as cold as ice. He couldn't run – his feet were stuck in the mud. No – he looked down – there was no mud. His feet were standing on a path. He just couldn't lift them up and move them.

He clenched his fingers around the stick. He was going to be sick. But the smell would cling to his stomach and all the rest of his organs, and it would pull them out as he vomited onto the path. He would sick up his liver and his lungs and his kidneys and all his miles and miles of intestines, and they would sink into the ground just like his feet and he would never get out of here.

But then there wasn't any point in going back out of the shadow anyway. The whole quest was fruitless, and not even the stick was good enough, now. He might as well stay where he was. Or better still, step further into the shadows . . .

From the front of the house, Ori barked.

The sound echoed round the air, bounced into Danny's heart, and knocked the smell into pieces for an instant, like a well-thrown ball against a cricket stump.

Danny ripped his feet from the ground, and ran.

He burst back into the unshadowed world and flung himself down onto the tufted grass, panting.

The sky was losing the last of its light; he could only make out shapes on the beach, hunkering down against the rising storm. The wind yanked at his hair, his clothes, Ori's fur – but his dog stood over him, coat flattened and dancing at the tips, and she was warm and alive, and so was he.

Never again, he vowed. That was the last time. Whatever else I have to do, I can't go back into the shadows. Not ever.

'You're OK now,' said Ori. 'You've done it.'

Danny struggled up onto one elbow, and looked at the box in his hand. It was a small wooden casket with a pattern of twisted vines made from dull grey metal creeping over the lid. Not particularly beautiful. Danny had seen plenty of similar ones on knick-knack tables at jumble sales.

He opened it.

All it contained was a notebook.

He bit back an exasperated curse. Notebooks had been helpful in the past. Maybe this was *The Book of Shadows*, even. How convenient would that be, to find it ready-made in a witch's box?

He opened the notebook.

'*Herbs to Cure Gout*' read the title of the first page. Danny tried again, turning over to the second page. '*Herbs to Cure Piles*'. Piles of what?

Third page. '*Herbs to Cure Twinges in the Kneecap*'.

He turned them over, page after page, full of lists of herbs, lists of herbs, lists of herbs . . .

'Oh for – !'

He did swear then, letting the worst words he could think of come out of his mouth in a violent, despairing stream, and flung the book as far away from him as he could.

All that, for nothing. Lists of herbs.

Ori trotted off and brought the notebook back to him in her soggy jaws, wagging her tail in the dusk. Danny shook his head.

'I know you're a retriever and all,' he said, 'but that thing's useless. Let's go back to the others.'

He trudged back down to the beach. By the time he got there, the wind had blown up into a gale so strong that he could hardly open his eyes enough to see the sea. He could only hear its roar growing in fury as the wind continued to torment it.

'Cath?' he called.

'Here!'

They were close by, finding what shelter they could against the dunes. The dunes didn't break the wind, but they gave a solid bank to lean on as the gusts battered them backwards, and Danny slid down beside Cath, glad to have something to lie against.

'Any luck?' she asked, raising her voice against the wind.

'No. Just another useless stupid notebook!'

'Did you – ?' Cath trailed off, but Danny understood that she was asking about the old woman. He shook his head, and the wind roared in his ears.

'No,' was all he could say.

In the beginning of all this trouble, he'd seen an old man called Abel Korsakof die before his eyes. For a long time, he'd thought that was the worst thing a person could ever witness. Now he knew it wasn't even close.

The wind blew sand up, and it filled his eyes. The sounds of the sea were getting harder to place: the wind sent the roaring of the waves dancing all around him, so that his ears could only tell him he was surrounded by water.

A raindrop fell, fat and cold.

'Let's get out of the rain!' he yelled.

'Boat shed . . . up the beach.' Cath waved her arms. 'Not far.'

And for a second she was Cath again, scrambling to her feet, holding Barshin, leading the way. Danny reached around for Shimny and dragged her by the mane.

'Wait!' he called over the wind to Cath.

Cath's hand came swooping out towards him, reaching to grab at his jumper.

'Hold my sleeve,' she said, and set off fast. Danny stumbled trying to keep up with her, Shimny in one hand and Cath's sleeve in the other. Ori was by his side. He couldn't look down to see her, but he'd have known if she'd been left behind.

After a while, they reached the lee of a crumbling wooden wall. With a shrieking of old hinges, Cath yanked the door open against the wind, and then they were in a damp, musty-smelling space, protected from the wind and rain. Despite an occasional drip falling on his hair, Danny felt a bit warmer out of the snarling gale.

'Now what?' he said, when the stillness reminded him that he had the basic things he needed, and should be getting on with his task.

'You do what you want,' said Cath, letting the door slam behind her and cutting off the daylight. 'I'm knackered. I'm going to sleep.'

He heard her rustling in the darkness, making a nest out of her bundle of rags, then falling silent. As he sat by himself, Ori's nose pushed up into the crook of his armpit and he put his arm around her.

This was the end.

I wonder if Sammael will appear, thought Danny, and come to crow over me. I wonder if he'll push me under the shadows, so he can watch me die. Or maybe he's got a special patch of shadow that he'll use just for me.

It's not Sammael, he reminded himself. This is Tom. The shadows are being controlled by Tom.

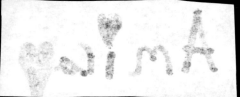

But he knew in his heart that whatever anyone else said – whatever stories they tried to tell him – Sammael was at the heart of all the badness in the world.

Ori pushed her head against him, and he reached for the stick, and told her his fears.

'Do you really think so?' she asked. 'Mightn't there be more to it than that?'

'I don't think so. I know so.' Danny smoothed his thumb along the crease between her ear and her head. 'However dark this night is, it's nothing compared to Sammael.'

'But the darkness –' said Ori '– isn't that where the colour lies?'

Danny's head began to hurt: a swift, clear pain behind his eyes, as though he'd been staring too long into a bright light. He felt suddenly exhausted, as though there was nowhere to go any more and he had hit a wall so thick and high that he couldn't begin to climb it.

If I had Isbjin al-Orr, he thought, we could leap over it together. That stag could jump as high as the moon.

Ori pushed her head into his ribs.

Danny snapped awake and opened his eyes. Daylight was shuffling in through the cracks in the walls and a small pane of cobwebbed glass at the back of the shed. He was tucked up against a corner, and the light was strong enough for him to see that in the middle sat an ancient boat, with Cath curled up inside it, Barshin in her arms. He had a moment of panic – Shimny wasn't there. But when he scrambled to his feet and threw open the door she was by the edge of the sea, head down, staring into the shallows.

The storm had gone, leaving the sea a dull grey, its surface shuddering like the skin of a horse against a fly's tiny legs.

Danny rubbed his arms to get some warmth into them and wandered down to the edge of the shore. He stood silently beside Shimny and watched as the water bubbled up towards his toes, but stepped back before it reached his shoes. There was no point in having wet feet so far from home.

His stomach gave an angry rumble, and he went back up the beach to the boat shed to see if Cath was awake.

She was sitting up in the boat with the small notebook in her hand, reading intently with a finger on the page.

'That stupid notebook,' said Danny. 'I should have chucked it in the sea.'

'Ssssh,' said Cath.

'Why? Have you reached the page of *"Herbs to Cure an Empty Stomach?"'*

As soon as he said it, he heard his cousin. It would be something Tom said – bounding from place to place, job to job, cow to cow, always hungry. Danny had never been that bothered about eating, though Aunt Kathleen's food was good. But Tom had been obsessed with it. He even knew which plants you could eat in the wild.

If only Tom were here. If only.

'Did you read it all?' asked Cath.

'Didn't need to. I got the gist.'

'So you didn't reach the stuff that wasn't about herbs, then?'

'What stuff?'

'Oh, you know, just stuff. About earth and fire and water and air. That sort of stuff.'

'Give it!' Danny leant forwards to snatch at the book but Cath whipped it away.

'No way. I'm not done.'

'Give it!' snapped Danny. 'I need it!'

'Should have read it before you chucked it away then, shouldn't you?' said Cath, standing up in the boat and holding the book out of Danny's reach. He swiped at it, but she was taller than him, and with the extra height from the bench inside the boat, he couldn't get near it.

Cath opened the book again, high above her head, and began to read.

'"*Otherwise known as the four classical elements, Earth, Fire, Water and Air – the things the ancient Greeks thought all other things were made of. The discovery of the chemical elements puts paid to this theory, but it is interesting to look at the classical elements in terms of Abstract Qualities.*" What's an abstract quality? She didn't half talk rubbish sometimes.'

'Please,' said Danny. 'If you're too thick to understand it, just give it to me.'

Cath looked down at him, a smirk on her greying face. For a second, he thought she was going to give him the book, but she continued to hold it high.

'Abstract qualities,' she said. 'Not things you can touch or hold or see or feel. Invisible things. Like the characters of people.'

Danny scrambled up onto the side of the boat, using Cath's jumper to pull himself up to her height. The rotten wood broke under his feet and they fell together, landing in a painful heap only slightly cushioned by Cath's bundle of rags. Danny's spine shuddered; for a second he lay stunned as a landed fish and then he grabbed Cath's wrist before she could whip the notebook out of his reach again.

Not caring if he was hurting her, he knelt on her arms and twisted it out of her grip.

He sat back against the broken side of the boat. Cath got up, rubbing her wrists, but Danny ignored her and read.

'"*Abstract qualities. Earth – stable, resilient, strong. Grounding. Water – fluid, imaginative, emotional. Escapist. Air – change, energy, yellow. A howling dog. Fire – assertiveness, passion, a roaring lion.*

'"*All my life I have thought of significance lying in threes. But last night I dreamed of a four-leafed clover, and this morning when I woke, it struck me what a balance there was in fours. Four are the seasons of the year – spring, summer, autumn and winter. Four are the points of the compass – North, South, East and West. And four are the corners of a book. Earth, Air, Fire and Water. These elements are not the building blocks of the world. They are four friends on a celestial journey, each one reliant upon the others. One day, when the four friends split apart, it will signify the end of the world.*"'

Danny turned the page. There was a list entitled '*Herbs to Cure Twinges in the Cartilage*'. The old woman seemed to have to run out of ramblings.

He looked up at Cath. 'It's just a load of rubbish,' he said. 'Doesn't mean anything.'

'No,' said Cath. 'You'd never call us friends, would you?'

Danny felt his cheeks go red. He tried to wish them pale again, but they burnt all the more. Cath sneered.

'Calm down,' she said. 'I ain't asking you to be my boyfriend. The four of us, I mean. Barshin. Me. That dog. And you.'

Danny stared at Ori and Barshin in turn. 'What about Shimny?' he said, remembering the horse, staring miserably at the sea outside.

'Yeah, I wondered about her. But she's dead, ain't she? She's made of something else, now, and we're just using her to get what we want. Maybe she was your friend, once, but that's just a memory now, ain't it? She ain't with you because she wants to help with the shadows.'

Danny choked. That wasn't true! Shimny must want to help them – she could run away, if she didn't want to. He never tied her up.

But he had promised to find her a home, and give her peace. And that was a hold as tight as any rope, for her.

Cath must have seen distress on his face and taken pity on him because she said, in an unusually gentle tone, 'Maybe think about it this way: the shadows can't get to her any more, so they don't affect her – it's the rest of us who are alive, and who need the shadows to stop. So if we're making a weapon against them, it's going to be made from something the four of us can get together. Don't you reckon?'

Danny looked at them again – Cath, Barshin and Ori.

The wind flipped the door of the boatshed shut with a loud clap, closing them in, and Shimny out.

Inside, the air stopped moving.

Four, Danny thought. Two animals, two people. Two wild creatures – Cath and Barshin, and two tame ones – Ori and me. Two girls – Ori and Cath, and two boys – Barshin and me. Every colour of fur and hair and skin between us. We're all so different, and yet we're together. I bet there isn't a thing in the world that one of us hasn't thought or won't one day think. We are everything it's possible to be.

Earth. Air. Fire. Water.

'Which one is which?' he said.

'I am the air,' said Ori. 'I feel my way through the world by reading the words that the air brings into my nose. I am the yellow dog, who howls in the night when I smell the souls of those arriving and departing the world going past me in every direction. The air is my sacred text; I read its every letter and punctuation mark.'

Barshin sat with his paws together, ears upright. Danny took the stick and directed his thoughts towards the hare.

'Did you hear me read? What are you?'

'Of course I heard,' said Barshin. 'I can always understand you, you know. I am the earth. I scent the air, and I listen to the water, and I feel the heat of fire. But it is the earth I read; the soil that lies upon it, and the plants that grow from it and the insects that crawl over it. When I am afraid, I press myself close to the earth. I understand that I am nothing but a piece of Earth temporarily separated from it, and one day I will return to it again.'

'It makes sense,' said Danny. 'You're the right colour.'

And although he couldn't bring himself to like Barshin, he saw that the hare was not his enemy any more. Their hearts were just made of different materials, and it would be very hard ever to understand each other, simply because of that.

But I need the earth, Danny thought. We all need the earth. It doesn't need us in return, it won't go offering solutions to our stupid mistakes. But we need it.

He turned to Cath.

'Ain't hard, is it?' she said. 'I reckon I'm fire. I can't say stuff like Barshin, and I don't know what your dog said to you, but all my life I've been burning – all the stupid stuff that happens, the stupid people that try to hurt you – I ain't ever felt like I'd sit down and take it. I burnt for Chromos, when I went there. I burnt for my house. I burnt to know everything Ida knew, to go up into the woods and hills and out onto the sea. Nothing in me ever stopped burning. Except –'

A grey flush spread over her cheeks, the colour of ashes.

'Except – maybe – I was fire. And maybe when the shadows came –'

'No,' said Danny. 'It's an element, no shadow can change that.'

'But fire gets put out, don't it?' said Cath. 'Fire dies.'

'You're not dead,' said Danny firmly. 'You're alive and breathing. You're still alight.'

Cath's lips stayed together and she bent her head a little, neither agreeing or disagreeing.

'So I must be water,' said Danny. It made sense: water took his fears away. He had galloped into the sea on Isbjin al-Orr,

121

and he'd thought it had been the stag who had made him feel strong and unafraid. But perhaps it had really been the water. Perhaps that was why Ori was right – he still wasn't afraid of the sea, even though he'd nearly drowned in it.

' But . . . I'm none of these things she said about water.' He gestured to the old woman's book. 'Imaginative. Escapist. I'm none of these things. Maybe I'm not the fourth bit here at all. Maybe it's you three and someone else.'

As he said it, he knew it must be true. The real fourth element would have been brave and questing, and made none of the stupid mistakes that he, Danny, had made. There was a bit that was missing, and it was still missing. It wasn't him.

'Don't be daft,' said Cath. 'Of course you're water. You're so bloomin' wet that you'd have to be.'

Danny looked at her. It was so easy for Cath. She just knew things. He never felt sure about anything. If they were back at home, in real life, at school, he was pretty sure they wouldn't even look at each other in the corridor.

For a second, he saw them all very far away, three other creatures sitting in a boatshed around the wreckage of a broken, rotten old boat, engaged on a desperate quest. Was he even there with them? Or did he belong back in the normal world, eating dinner and watching TV and hanging around on the sidelines of the football pitch?

But where he belonged wasn't important right now. The only thing that mattered was that he was here, together with the three others. Earth, air, fire. And water.

'So what do we need to do?' he asked.

Chapter 13

Four Stories

Barshin flicked his ears solemnly. 'We need to collect ourselves into a book. Any book will do – maybe just make a notebook out of the blank pages left in Ida's book. And then we need to think – how would we define ourselves?'

'I'm a boy,' said Danny. 'I'm thirteen. Er . . . brown hair . . .'

'No, no,' explained Barshin. 'We should ask – what is in us that has brought us here, together? That bond is what we need to capture. If we can explain how we came to be here, the stories, once bound together, will contain the power to push us into the world of Mab. Don't you see?'

Danny swallowed. 'Not really.'

'We think of what we all want,' said Cath. 'We put the things together. If the world's made of four elements and we're the four elements, then the things we want must be the future hopes of all the world. Get it?'

Danny thought about it. 'Nope.'

He asked Ori.

'The most powerful part of us,' said Ori, 'is our hope. If we hope for the same things, we can make them happen. We need to find out what we're hoping for.'

And Danny got it.

'Well, then,' said Barshin. 'What's brought us here?'

They repeated the question among themselves, and to each other.

'I think,' said Ori, looking around wisely, 'that it is loss. We all have the look of creatures who have lost something, and who know that it is unlikely that we will ever find those things again. But we know in our hearts that we will keep hoping against hope to find them. Am I correct?'

'Maybe,' said Danny. He asked the others.

'A hare I loved was taken from me,' said Barshin. 'And Cath?'

Cath scowled. 'I ain't lost nobody,' she said. 'Nobody I needed.'

'Ori didn't say you had to need what you lost,' said Danny. 'She just said that you've lost it, and you know you'll probably never find it again. It's a family for you, isn't it?'

'No,' said Cath. 'I never lost one. I never had one.'

Danny raised an eyebrow at her. 'Now who's not listening?' he said.

Cath clenched her fists, and shook her head.

Danny turned back to Ori. 'What have you lost, then?'

'Tennis balls,' said Ori. 'Owners. Bones. Trails of scent.'

'Anything serious?'

She put her head on one side, gazing at him, unblinking.

'My home,' she said.

For once, her tone wasn't soft and merry. Danny felt it blame him, and he didn't want to know why.

Ori carried on. 'And you have lost your cousin. So that makes all of us, doesn't it?'

'I guess so,' Danny agreed. 'But do you really think that four small lost things are enough to make *The Book of Shadows*? It doesn't seem much.'

'Try it,' said Ori.

Danny looked at the notebook. There were a few pages left – six, exactly – and a thin pencil tucked down inside the spine. He tore out the blank pages and rested them on the book.

'Go on, then,' he said to Barshin. 'Tell me yours. I'll write.'

Barshin closed his eyes. 'I will find her on a summer's morning,' he said. 'At the foot of the old beech tree in the land by the lazy-flowing stream. She will have our young with her, the young that she was to have had that spring – and they will be fine young leverets, only partly grown, but bold enough to roam from her side. She will wait in the morning mist, and I will know from the curve of her crouched back that it can be no other hare. And when she sees me, she will lay back her ears and spring up into a boxing stance, and we will fly at each other, our hind feet punching the earth, and we will fight and cuff, and lunge at each other's necks until our legs and paws are so tangled that we can do nothing but fall onto the earth in a wrestle. And I will be a creature with my own life, and nothing else will ever matter to me.'

The hare opened his eyes.

'That it?' asked Danny. 'That's all?'

'Do the dreams of another creature seem small to you?' asked Barshin. 'It isn't the time to scorn me for my lack of ambition, you know.'

'No, I wasn't,' said Danny, hastily. 'It just doesn't sound like great magic.'

'Well, it's an impossible dream,' snapped Barshin. 'I've just described the happening of something impossible. If that doesn't fit in with your definition of magic, I suggest you come up with a better idea yourself.'

'Sorry,' said Danny.

But Barshin crouched down in the boat, and stared off into space, ignoring him.

'Ori?' Danny turned to his dog, wanting comfort. 'What do you want to put in the book?'

Ori cocked her head first to one side and then the other. Even with the strengthening morning light filtering in through the cracks in the walls of the shed, her golden coat seemed dull and dark.

'The old man is walking under the railway bridge next to the canal, calling my name. I can hear him from a long way off, even though his voice is quiet and old. And I leave everything behind – the rabbit-holes, the day-old chicken bones, the voices in the air, and I rush back to him, and fall into step by his side, and we go home.'

Danny waited, sure that there must be more. But Ori's tone was quiet and bland, and no other words came.

'Is that it?' he said, before he could stop himself.

'That,' said the dog, 'is it.'

Danny felt a pang of jealousy. Wasn't she his dog? Now she seemed to want some other master, some old man.

Ori looked up at him. 'I will always stay with you,' she said. 'We are bound together, you and I. But I had another home, once, and I will never see it again. It is impossible now.'

'You can go back if you like,' said Danny, a spiny lump rising in his throat. 'After this is over.'

'No,' said Ori. 'You needn't worry. I can't go back, none of us can. Even if we manage to open the world of Mab for you, we will all still live in Xur's world, and these things will never come true for us. There is only one direction in this world: forward.'

She said it with such finality that Danny didn't dare ask any more. He turned away from the huge gap that suddenly lay between them, not wanting to look into its darkness.

I wish I'd never asked, he thought. I wish she'd been born into my arms, and knew nothing else.

And as he looked at Cath, he heard Ori stand and move her bulk over to his side, and he felt her soft fur against the skin of his ankle, where his sock had fallen down.

'Go on, then,' he said to Cath.

'I ain't got nothing to put in there,' said Cath. 'You're wrong. I ain't lost nothing.'

'But you have,' said Danny, irritation picking at him like a nettle barb. Why couldn't she just get it done, like the other two?

'No way,' said Cath. 'I never had a mum. Same as I never had a dad, just some fat git who couldn't be bothered with me. I ain't gonna tell you some story about how in my dreams we're all living together in one happy little family. My dad was horrible. My mum didn't want him or me. I don't want her or him.'

'But don't you wish you had a family,' said Danny. 'One who looked after you, and made you happy?'

Cath shook her head. 'Families don't make you happy. I'm fine without one.'

'You're lying,' said Danny. 'Everybody wants a family. A good family, I mean.'

'What, like yours?' Cath curled her lip. 'Nah, you can keep 'em.'

Danny looked at her. More shadows would be up in the skies, rolling. They needed to get going.

Cath stared back. Her jaw was clenched tight, her grey eyes sunk into the dark sockets of her grey face. She was silent.

'Oh for God's sake!' Danny thrust the paper at her. 'You do it, then. Write anything. Whatever you like. You can still write, can't you?'

Cath took the pencil from his hand and flexed her fingers around it. 'You have to promise not to read it. Ever.'

'I promise,' said Danny.

'Put your hands where I can see them.'

He spread his hands in front of him, so that she could see none of his fingers were crossed.

'I promise,' he said, flexing his fingers in the gloom. 'I promise I won't ever read what you write. Just write it.'

She wrote for a couple of minutes, her hand slow and laboured, the paper curling around her knee. Once or twice she looked up at Danny to check he wasn't peeking. Danny pretended to find the crumbling shed walls as interesting as Barshin and Ori clearly thought they were.

It was strange, what Cath had said about them all fitting together. The more time they all spent together, the more Danny realised how little he knew about any of them.

At last Cath handed back the paper to him. She'd covered the page with a blank piece.

'If you read it, I'll kill you,' she said.

He wondered if it was anything to do with him, but Cath wasn't going red, or avoiding his gaze, so it probably wasn't. She just didn't want him to know her secrets.

He wanted to know them.

Swallowing, he forced his thoughts back to his own story. What was he going to put into *The Book of Shadows*? So far, it had a dead hare, a lost old man, and a complete unknown. He didn't have to come up with anything grand to compete with that.

But as he tried to think about the worst thing he'd ever lost, the light seemed to recede from the cracks and the boatshed grew duller and gloomier.

His heart snatched at his ribs. Could it be more shadows? Was another lot coming over, stifling out the last of the natural sky along this beach?

Cath was watching him. Barshin was watching him. Ori was watching him.

'I think the shadows are coming,' he said, his throat dry.

'No, they're not,' said Barshin. 'You just don't want to write, that's all.'

'No, they're not,' said Ori. 'It's just hard to think of the impossible. You have to fight the bit of you that says there's no point.'

And that, thought Danny, was the difference between them. Barshin thought Danny was weak, and had no patience with him. Ori wanted to help, and be gentle.

He pushed himself to his feet and went outside. Barshin and Ori were right – the clouds were still pale, drifting thickly over the sea. The sea itself was cold and grey, with a hard shine to it, lapping at the gritty beach with dirty tongues of foam. A breeze trailed faintly through the air, but nothing much else was moving apart from a flock of gulls further up the shore.

They had walked a fair distance in the storm. Danny saw the mushroom of shadow-cloud over the house was a good way off, now. He was safe here. But as more and more clouds came, the unshadowed land would grow smaller and smaller, until it was impossible to escape.

He turned his back on the clouds and the shadows and looked out to sea. It came upon him very strongly that the sea, one day, would be the place where he died. He wouldn't go in his bed like an old man, or come to a lingering end in a hospital ward. For him it would be the rolling waves of the sea, rising up to claim him for their own.

But I'll be old by then, he told himself. And it seemed like such a good thing – a natural thing – a thing to look forward to, almost – that his heart glowed warm and happy at the thought of it. I'll live all my life, he thought. Each bit of it, right to the end, will be interesting and strange and worth living. All sorts of things might happen to me, but I'll never be bored.

Danny found himself smiling. It was hard to think of the impossible, because *this* was the impossible, and it was happening. Most of the time he hated it. But sometimes the clouds came apart, and he forgot Tom and Sammael, and he was just himself. And the impossible things came alive in his hands.

He thought about what he'd lost. It was obvious, really. Tom. And, temporarily, his parents. But he'd lost other things too. Shimny. His security. He'd even lost a sister once, long ago.

Should his story be about Emma? No, the loss that had brought him to the boathouse was specifically the loss of Tom. Tom's story – Tom's death – was his purpose. Emma was just a lurking shadow, too big for him to look at.

He began the story of Tom. 'Once, I had a cousin,' he wrote. 'He lived on a farm at Sopper's Edge, and he liked badgers and birds and cows and Hangman's Wood and the horses Apple and Shimny . . .'

He paused. He hadn't words to express his longing for Tom – the knowledge that he'd spent all those days hanging around with him on the farm, a bit bored, not appreciating any of it, and just too late he'd come to understand how much fun he'd actually been having. How many other boys had galloped horses over the hill in the silver moonlight? How many others had been taken to watch kestrels, or fought battles with caber-sized fence posts, or been thrown head first into slimy ponds?

He nearly choked at the thought that it was all gone, and would never happen again. He couldn't write another word.

So he drew Tom. Tom on the farm, and all the things he had loved around him – horses, calves, sheep, fields, beetles, weasels, buzzards, rye grass and timothy, coltsfoot and clover, Aunt Kathleen and Sophie and the fences and the tractor and the cow byres, and as he drew them, he realised how much Tom had shown him of the world that he would never otherwise have known.

I need him back, thought Danny. He was my cousin. I let him die.

It was a good drawing. Anyone looking at it would have said, 'Is that all? That's not so impossible, surely?'

But it would never happen again.

Cath sawed off a length of her tangled hair with a piece of rusty metal lying in the corner of the shed and made a long, thin plait of it, feeding in strands at a time. Danny used the pencil to punch two holes in the pages, and found a scrap of sailcloth to wrap around the outside. Ancient and stiff with salt, it was just about the right size and shape for a cover.

'Here.'

Cath found a better awl – a thick sail needle, blunted with rust, and Danny managed to push it through the sailcloth until the holes were big enough for the hair string.

And so it was bound together. It looked a mess – a small, scruffy bit of yellow-brown cloth, hanging stiffly over a few pieces of raggedly torn paper – but it was a book; they had made *The Book of Shadows*, and on this deserted beach it seemed only right that it appeared as a thing just washed up by the sea.

Chapter 14

The First Shadow

They gathered round the book and watched it, expectantly, but it was still nothing more than a few scraps of paper.

'What do we do now?' asked Danny. 'We've made it. It's got all our hopes in it. Do I just write, and things come true?'

'Remember the story,' said Barshin. 'We need to take it back to the place where it all began: the shadow that Xur threw Mab's world into. Only then will it come alive.'

'But how are we supposed to find that? It must have disappeared thousands of years ago. Millions of years ago.'

'Ah, but this is a new book. And shadows move.'

Danny rolled his eyes. 'Stop being cryptic. If you want to tell me something, just say it in words I'll understand. We haven't got much time.'

'Yeah,' said Cath. 'Don't leave it to him to work out. We'll be here till the sun turns into a Christmas tree.'

Barshin let their comments fly away into silence. 'Well,

Cath was right – stories are stories, not the truth. But even so, there's usually some truth lurking somewhere. In the story of Mab and Xur, there's a moment when the world could have become one thing, and instead became another. Without knowing anything about where Mab and Xur stood, we can still know that our own lives are full of such moments. Mine is. Yours is. And you made this *Book of Shadows*. There must have been a moment when something huge happened to you, which shaped your entire life. I'd think that is the place you need to find. Where did your road fork?'

'Well, it does that all the time,' said Danny. 'Every time I do anything, I could always have done something else, couldn't I?'

'I'm not talking about the small things,' said Barshin. 'I mean the ones that completely shape your life.'

Danny ran through what he could remember of his entire life in his head. He didn't remember anything from the first three years. What if something had happened then that no one had told him about? He'd never know where his road had forked in the time that he couldn't remember.

'Come on, get on with it,' said Cath. 'We've got to go.'

She coughed, a harsh wheeze of breath rattling at her chest.

'Why?' For a second Danny let himself be distracted.

'They'll come back. They are coming back. I can feel it.'

Danny didn't question this. She was so grey now that she could probably hear all the clouds, wherever they were.

He stood in the doorway of the boat shed. Shimny was still in the same position: head down, nose grazing the sand. Shimny, who'd raced along a hilltop, who'd fallen down a quarry side with him, standing in hopeless despair. She'd probably been like that all through the storm.

Storms. Trees waving wildly in the gale. Trees falling.

Trees being struck by lightning. Breaking, cleaving in two, right down to the smoking earth.

Trees dying.

People dying.

Children dying, and other children being born. To replace them.

Of course. Emma. He couldn't remember the accident, because it had happened before he'd even been born, but without it his parents would never have had him. His first fork had been Emma's death.

'Emma,' he said abruptly.

'Who?'

'Emma. My older sister. She died in a storm, before I was born. That's where my shadow would be – with Emma. But I don't know where she's buried. We never go there.'

'Your parents never tell you?' said Cath.

'Nope. They don't like to talk about her,' said Danny.

'Jeez,' said Cath. 'Your perfect little family.'

She looked at him, her face set. She was as grey as she'd been when he'd pulled her out of the house.

'You need the yellow flowers,' he said. 'The gorse. Wait, I'll get you some.'

'I need to get out of here,' said Cath.

* * *

He ran back to the dunes to get some gorse, pushing some of the spiny plant into Cath's hands. She didn't throw it away, but stood, waiting for his next action. They were all waiting for him to tell them what he was going to do. How he was going to find Emma's grave.

He had no idea.

Go into Chromos and wish to find it? But he couldn't. Cath couldn't. Barshin couldn't. If they tried to go again in their current states, Chromos would be grey and unbearable.

'I can go,' said Ori. 'I can get up on Shimny and go in, and find out for you.'

Danny was dubious. 'Are you sure? How will you know what to see? You don't know anything about Emma.'

'I know enough about your heart,' said Ori. 'I'll find a way.'

Danny looked at her gazing back up at him with her deep brown eyes. Had anyone ever had such a loyal dog? He smiled, and realised that he hadn't smiled for a long time.

'Thanks,' he said. 'Thanks for trying. I don't think it'll work, but thanks.'

'It might,' said Ori. 'Help me up onto Shimny's back and tell her where to go.'

Shimny's back was cold and narrow, and her ribs were as hard as the struts of the broken boat. Danny boosted Ori up and the dog perched across the horse's bony spine.

'I thought she was supposed to be a ghost,' muttered Cath. 'Not a blooming xylophone.'

Shimny didn't hear, or, if she heard, her misery was so deep that nothing could add to it. She barely acknowledged Danny's promises of a home, of rest, of a sanctuary, but agreed to go without any gladness.

They watched dog and horse jump up into the sky and become harder to see, until it was impossible to separate Ori and Shimny from their background, and Danny knew they had dissolved into Chromos. He felt a pang of loss, but there was warmth in his chest at the thought that Ori might go into Chromos and see for him. What a dog to have. What a friend.

He kept his eyes fixed on the spot where he had last seen a fragment of her, and waited for her to come back.

Danny couldn't say how much time passed before they returned, only that the day grew old and the evening shadows lengthened, but the skies above the beach stayed clear. The light faded and his eyes grew tired, but he stared out towards the place where Ori and Shimny had disappeared, and he tried to imagine what might be happening to them.

Cath and Barshin roamed about the beach and brought him things to eat: raw seaweed that was so salty it took the skin off his lips; glistening fleshy blobs excavated from their shells, which he swallowed down without examining. He didn't want to know what they were. At least they filled his growling stomach.

And then, as he began to fear that night would fall and Ori would still be gone, the wind picked up and the waves leapt a little, and he saw a black-and-white leg appear in the low sky over the sea.

They landed in a swift rush, looming out of the air and surging towards him, and Danny put up his hands – to protect himself, to show his delight, or because he wanted to throw them around Ori, he didn't know which – and Shimny came to a halt before him.

Ori leapt down from her back, tail wagging, pushing her head into Danny's palm.

'Did you see it?' was all he could ask.

'Yes! Of course I did! I told you I would, didn't I?'

'Where?' asked Danny. 'Where, exactly?'

'There are some woods, not far from where you live. Emma wasn't buried, but your parents scattered her ashes in a clearing, under a big oak tree. It is just out of town . . .'

Danny knew where it was. The place he'd first seen Isbjin al-Orr. Of course.

It was a nature reserve he'd often visited with his parents. They'd never said anything about Emma being there, but they'd taken him for walks, shown him all the little paths and tracks that criss-crossed the small woodland, sat down with him to eat picnics in hidden clearings. It was the first place he'd thought of when he'd wanted to bury the stick, hoping somehow that it might be reclaimed by ordinary nature. And then he'd gone back there to get the stick back and seen the stag in the silver moonlight, and everything had spiralled out of control again.

It was an enchanted place. A shadowed place.

Emma's place.

'But it's all the way back home,' he said, still slow with the wonder of remembering. 'We can't go back through Chromos because of the grey . . . we'll have to go on earth, and I don't know the way, or even how far it is. Just that it's very far . . .'

'But I can go through Chromos,' said Ori. 'I can imagine it, and steer Shimny there. Can't you all sit on Shimny's back with your eyes closed while I guide her?'

Danny frowned, looking at the horse. 'It wouldn't work . . .'

'Come on,' said Ori. 'You thought it wouldn't work last time, but it did, didn't it? Couldn't you put your trust in me? I'd save you from anything.'

'Maybe. But what about them?' Danny looked at Cath and Barshin. Terror plucked at his chest as he imagined setting off without Cath's strength or Barshin's wisdom.

'If you all could close your eyes and trust me,' said Ori, 'then I think we'd do it. We all want to get there, don't we?'

Danny turned to Cath. 'Could you go through Chromos with your eyes closed?'

'Ah,' said Barshin. 'You mean, like Orpheus in the underworld? Not to look, on pain of losing all that you most want? I could do it.'

'I asked Cath,' said Danny.

Cath was silent, gazing down at the sand. Danny wished he knew more about what she thought. She was strong enough to do anything. Why would she hesitate at this?

At last she looked out to sea. 'I could,' she said. 'I'd go even greyer. But I could do it.'

'Why would you go greyer?'

Cath rolled her eyes. 'You'll never get it,' she said. 'Chromos is just a means to an end, for you. For me, it's the whole world.'

Danny wanted to argue with her, but there wasn't time for anything now, except getting back to the woods and making *The Book of Shadows* work, and setting Tom's soul free. He clambered up onto Shimny's back and helped the rest of them up. Ori sat at the front, between Shimny's shoulders, and stared forward.

'Bury your face in me,' she advised Danny. 'And Cath should put hers against Barshin's fur.'

'We won't be able to breathe,' said Danny.

'Perhaps that might be a good thing,' said Ori. 'Perhaps, the less of Chromos you let into your senses, the less you'll want to look at it.'

As they climbed up into the land of colours, Danny felt it singing to him, warm and green. Open your eyes, his heart said, beating strongly. Let yourself back into Chromos.

He pushed his face further into Ori's fur and concentrated on her earthy, greasy smell. Ori, he thought. Ori, my friend. I trust you, and I will not look.

Cath felt the wind stir into a great gale; it blew around her ears, tugging at her hair. Come and dance with me, it said. Come and run wild through the mountains.

No, she answered it miserably, her heart hard. Just when I thought there was nothing more for me to lose, they've taken the last bit of freedom from me. I'm not allowed to look at Chromos. This is as bad as the world can ever get.

But one day, the wind said, you'll come back here and you'll fly free forever.

And it let her go.

Night rolled over as they travelled, and gave way to a pale, raw morning. As the last wisps of Chromos fled away, Shimny plodded back onto the Earth again and they arrived at the road that ran past the nature reserve. There were no cars about, only a few frozen birds and an edge of winter sun. They left Shimny at the gate and started up the narrow forest path.

Danny wasn't thinking of Emma as he made his way towards the clearing. He was thinking of the first time he and Cath had been here together, when he'd persuaded Isbjin al-Orr and the doe, Teilin, to take them on their journey.

'Cold, ain't it?' said Cath, rubbing her arms. She had her bundle of rags draped around her neck and shoulders, but she was shivering.

The last dead leaves clung to the branches of the trees. There wasn't enough sunlight for shadows here; the weak, white day filtered gloomily through the treetops, and the woodland floor was silent.

Danny came into the clearing and looked around. It was just a space between some trees in a muddy little patch of tattered scrub. There was no sign of the hole he'd dug under the tree when he'd buried the stick, of course. The woodland had long since filled it in, and pushed out all traces of him.

White sky. Mottled brown earth. Trees, lichens, mosses, fungi and decaying leaves. No brightness, no darkness. Hardly the border between two worlds.

The four of them stood in the chilly wind. Even Ori's luxurious coat looked shabby as the breeze picked at it. Her eyes were running; two teardrops of gummed-up hair dribbled towards her jowls. Barshin's fur had faded again to a moth-eaten grey. Cath was filthy, her torn clothes long outgrown.

Danny took out *The Book of Shadows* and stood with it in his hand, waiting for something to happen.

Somewhere, in a distant corner of his mind, he heard Sammael laughing at him.

'You don't know what you're doing,' sneered the jeering creature. 'You can't do anything by yourself. Pathetic.'

Except I can, thought Danny. Because I have a taro.

He took the stick from his pocket and laid it over the sailcloth cover. It was a natural, thoughtless gesture and he wasn't expecting anything to happen, but almost at once the stick lost its hardness and sagged softly into the sailcloth, pressing itself into the material.

Danny crouched at the foot of the oak tree and placed the book on the ground. He put both hands on the stick and pressed. His fingers sunk in, as if it were made of plasticine. When he pulled them away there were two rows of dents on the stick. He could mould it. It was asking him to make something else out of it.

And then he remembered. The cover of *The Book of Storms* had been a taro, hadn't it? Sammael had hammered out a taro and wrapped it around the pages, and the book had given him the power to write Danny's movements – to write him galloping along a hilltop on Shimny, to write them falling into a quarry . . .

Now it's my turn, thought Danny in grim delight. Now it's my turn to write for him.

He stretched out the stick, smoothing it between his fingers. It never felt as if it would break, but it was a slow process, because sometimes it wanted to recoil from the stretching and contract back into its original shape. Then he would mutter a curse, and remember what he was trying to do, and stretch it out patiently again until it agreed to hold. He never looked up at the others, although he knew they were watching him.

At last, it was done. Stretched, the stick kept its brown, woody colour, but when he wrapped it around the sailcloth, it went black. He didn't have to untie the string of Cath's hair and fix it on – it stuck by itself to the cloth, tucking itself neatly around the edges, holding to a square shape at the corners.

Danny held it, suddenly afraid of the quiet around him. Had he lost his power to speak to everything, by using the taro for something else?

'Ori?' he said.

'I'm here,' answered the dog, and he knew it was OK. He hadn't lost anything. He had made something new.

And there was only one thought in his head.

'Where's Sammael?' he said, looking up at Barshin. 'I'm going to kill him.'

Chapter 15

Playing with Shadows

'The shadows,' said Barshin. 'You have to stop the shadows first.'

'Right,' said Danny, and he opened the book, took Ida's pencil from the remains of her notebook, and wrote, '*And then there were no more shadows.*'

The world vanished into scorching white light. Cath screamed: a horrible, deathly howl of pain, and before Danny could see what was happening to her, his vision disappeared, and he had to throw his arm around his face to shield it from the blinding whiteness and the burning heat, and he was struggling to breathe, gasping for cool air.

His shaking hands did the job for him – they scribbled out the words he'd just written, gouging a hole in the page, and fumbled out new words underneath.

'*The shadows came back.*'

The world sank into bleak normality. It happened quickly enough, but before he looked at his friends, Danny scribbled, '*Cath, Barshin, Ori, Danny and Shimny were OK*'.

'Idiot,' said Cath. The familiarity of the word was oddly comforting. Danny didn't disagree with her.

'OK,' said Barshin. 'I think we've established that whatever you just wrote, it wasn't a good idea. What did you write?'

'Just that there weren't any more shadows,' said Danny, his cheeks going red again. 'I thought it'd know what I meant.'

'Idiot,' said Cath again. She rubbed her eyes.

'Quite,' said Barshin. 'Apparently some shadows are necessary. They seem to filter the sunlight to a bearable level.'

Danny bit back a rude word and took a deep breath. He couldn't argue with that.

'OK,' he said, looking at the book lying like a slab of explosive in his hand. Then he put the pencil point down against its page once more. What could he try that wouldn't do anyone any harm?

He wrote '*a bluebird appeared*'– just because it was the first thing he could think of – and there it was in front of him, hopping over the woodland clearing. A bluebird.

It hopped twice and pecked at a fragment of something. A real, small bird, the colour of the sky in Chromos.

The book trembled in his hands, rough bark wriggling against his palms.

Use me, it said. I am yours. Use me. Don't be afraid. Make the world again, exactly how you want it.

Danny stared at the bluebird for a moment longer. Then he readjusted his hold on the pencil and wrote: '*Tom's soul found peace.*'

The air released a gentle puff of wind. Would it blow away the shadows?

'*They raced to the* –' he wrote, and then scribbled out '*They*', and replaced it with '*Cath, Barshin, Ori, Danny and Shimny – raced to the top of the hill, where they could* –'

He saw with alarm that the page was starting to fill up, and tried to keep his handwriting small – '*watch the town.*'

And they were racing – back to Shimny, dragging her with them – all five of them in crazy leaps and bounds across roads and fields, over hedges and around trees. Cath caught her foot on a stone wall and fell head first over it, grazing her face and hands. Barshin threw himself at a five-barred gate and misjudged its height, crashing against the top rail. Ori dodged a car and ran into a tree on the roadside, and Danny stumbled into a fly-tipped fridge, but they all got up again and ran on, couldn't stop running, couldn't think to slow down. Only Shimny kept her head low, lost in her dark misery, steadily plodding after the other four as they capered on.

Danny had written it, and it had to happen now. He kept tight hold of the pencil. He could stop them just by writing '*They stopped*' but he was running too fast to write – he had written himself out of his own control.

Sammael would be laughing at me, he thought, as he hurdled a bench and dodged around the bus stop. But it's only a small mistake. It won't hurt me. I'll get to the top of the hill, then I'll watch the shadows clear from the town and know not to write myself into the story in future. I'll stay in control. The story will just be about Sammael, and how he dies.

And he scrambled through a hedge, not feeling the hundreds of tiny thorns that raked his skin, and the top of the hill was in sight, and he looked forward to the view.

They came to a stumbling, scratched halt, and stood together, looking down over the patchily-shadowed town.

'Jeez,' gasped Cath, breathing hard. 'What was that?'

Danny nodded. 'Sorry. It was the book. It takes things kind of – literally.'

'Maybe be a bit more specific next time?' said Cath. 'I mean, maybe just say fly, or something?'

Danny wanted to thrust the book at her and tell her she could do it herself, if she knew so much better. But it was definitely his book. No one else could touch the taro. She was irritatingly right, though – flying would have been a much better idea. Danny had still been thinking in normal, practical terms.

But what did it matter? The shadows were about to disappear.

He stood and waited.

And waited.

The clouds stayed still.

The shadows stayed still.

Danny looked at the book to check. Yes, he had written it exactly as he'd thought – '*Tom's soul found peace*'. But nothing was happening.

Perhaps Tom's soul needed to collect up the shadows. Danny didn't dare write anything specifically about shadows again.

He tried: '*And all the effects of Tom's torment were lifted from the earth*'.

Something happened to the breeze: it shifted, realigned itself, and Danny felt for a moment that he might be standing in the middle of an invisible game of Tetris, feeling the blocks tumbling and rearranging themselves around him.

But the clouds stayed, and the shadows stayed.

'Look!' Cath pointed towards the far horizon in the south, on the other side of the low valley. Clouds were bunching together in the distance – swooping, honing in on a fixed point. It was so far away that Danny knew they wouldn't be in danger, but he shuddered nonetheless. There were farms on the other side of the valley. Houses. Villages. People. Animals.

'Ain't you gonna stop them?' said Cath.

'I'm trying,' snapped Danny. 'It's not that easy.'

'Just write that they stop, dumbo.'

Danny clenched his fist around the pencil. 'You want to go blind again? No? Well, shut up then.'

'Shut up yourself,' said Cath. 'Just sort it out. You said you knew it was Tom.'

'It is,' said Danny. It took a strange effort to say the words, which made him wonder if he was doubting himself. He frowned. 'At least, I think so . . . It does sort of . . . feel . . . like it is . . . Don't you reckon?'

Cath's face was drained and grey. She thought for a moment.

'I don't know,' she said. '*You* said it was. Did you get it wrong?'

'No!' Danny flushed. 'No, I can't have! It must be him, I'm sure of it. I just haven't found the right thing to write, that's all.'

'Well, can't you write him here in front of you, then ask him?'

An uneasy claw picked at the nape of Danny's neck.

He ignored it. Of course! He could use the book to make Tom alive again! Then everything – completely everything – would be fine.

Tom, alive – !

He seized the edge of the book and wrote quickly: '*Tom came alive again*'.

The hillside stayed quiet as he scanned it eagerly for signs of Tom. The wind dropped.

And nothing came. Danny had a sudden vision of Tom, stuck in the airless atmosphere of the aether, brought back to life and struggling to breathe.

He wrote on, rapidly. '*Tom was on the hillside with Danny.*'

The air around him lurched sideways, as though the Earth, sailing through space, had struck an iceberg. Before him, the sky thinned and changed colour from white to peach, and then a figure was standing a few metres away, and Danny raised his eyes to it.

Tom.

Not Tom.

Horribly burnt, his blond hair reduced to a few black strands across his scalp. His eyes were empty sockets, his body a withered skeleton. Tom had fallen into a fire . . .

Danny couldn't look. He closed his eyes and turned away as bile rose in his gut and a pain tore across his chest.

151

Keeping his face averted, he tried to add to the sentence in the book. Something – anything – to get rid of whatever was standing in front of him.

'Tom was the same as he'd been before the fire –'

This time, he knew what the lurching was. It was the Earth and the air desperately trying to obey him, to conjure up his wish. They strained together to make something that neither of them contained. And they came up with –

Something that looked a little more like Tom. More hair. The hint of gentle blue eyes, sunk deeply into a still-haunted face.

Danny risked a small glance, and let it stay on Tom for a few moments. Not so bad. Maybe it was just a matter of building Tom again, bit by bit.

He opened his mouth to tell this to Cath, and couldn't see her.

Or Barshin. Or Ori. Or Shimny.

They had all gone.

An order of things had been reversed, or reset, to a time or situation before he'd met any of the others.

Without hesitating, Danny scribbled out the last sentences he'd written, and he kept scribbling until not a letter of them could be seen on the page. When he looked up, Tom was gone and the others were back.

'Where did you go?' he asked.

Cath shook her head. 'Nowhere,' she said. 'We're right here.'

'You did go. I wrote Tom back, just like he used to be, and you all disappeared.'

They stared at him.

He shrugged, helplessly. 'I don't think I can bring him back,' he said. 'Maybe Sammael has too much of him. Maybe it's . . . I don't know. I can feel the things – the earth and the air – trying to rearrange things . . . but they can't. I don't know why. I don't know what to write, so I can get to him, or stop all this . . .'

'OK,' said Cath. 'Write down that you know what to write, then.'

It was so simple. He opened his mouth to argue, then closed it again.

Of course she was right. Had Cath ever made a stupid suggestion?

He wrote: '*Danny knew what to do to stop the shadows.*'

Thoughts of Tom vanished from his head. For a second, he waited. Nothing was going to happen. The wind was picking up, but the hillside would stay exactly the same.

And then his head lifted and turned.

A long way off, the creature was racing low over a field, covering the ground with incredible speed. He knew that nobody but himself had seen it – it was so small that unless you knew exactly where it was, you couldn't possibly spot that it was there.

He followed its progress across the fields and tarmac roads, under the hedges, over the narrow streams.

It ran like quicksilver.

An animal. A normal, earthly animal, with greater speed than a cheetah. Or an express train. Or, Danny guessed, a jumbo jet.

It hared across the flat bottom of the valley, and his heart quickened.

It was coming towards them.

Did it know about him?

His stomach curled in fear. Only an animal – a tiny animal – but with what powers, it alone knew.

He glanced across at the others. Greyish Cath, greyish Barshin. He wished he had written them happy and healthy again. It should have been the first thing he did, instead of conjuring up that stupid bluebird. But all that would have to wait now.

The animal was bringing a shadow.

Curled up, held in its mouth . . . Danny saw the black patch, clamped between the tiny fangs of – of all things –

A stoat.

Chapter 16

The Stoat

Danny stood, paralysed, for another second, and then tried to begin writing. His hand shook so badly that he could barely hold it to the page.

'Danny knew the stoat's name – the one with the shadow in its mouth –' he wrote.

Iaco. The stoat was called Iaco.

'Iaco dropped the shadow.'

The stoat opened its tiny jaws and dropped the patch of shadow with an anguished shriek. As soon as the patch hit the ground, it unfurled. Clouds bunched and bucked in the sky, and a shadow fell over the scant sunlight.

'Iaco –'

Did what?

And then the stoat was in front of them, racing across their vision, and just as Danny was about to write another word, it kicked around and leapt in the air, dodging back on itself. A flash of white underbelly caught his eye, and he stared at it, held, fascinated by how fast it ran.

The stoat leapt, kinked, flashed up the white of its belly again. Four pairs of eyes held fast to her. It raced, left-to-right, right-to-left, left-to-right, in an unceasing whirlwind.

Right-to-left.

Left-to-right.

The white flash.

The brown back.

The white flash.

Danny's hand grew limp on the pencil.

White flash.

Brown back.

White.

Brown.

White.

Brown . . .

Cath jolted him sharply, and for a second his eyes flicked away as he tried to keep his balance. They went first to the green grass, then the grey sky. The shadows were racing up the hillside behind Iaco, racing up towards them all, about to swallow them all, except that flash of white and brown . . .

Danny grabbed the pencil and wrote firmly 'Iaco stopped. Iaco's shadows stopped.'

The stoat hit an invisible wall in mid air, then fell to the ground. The cloud ceased, mid-swoop, and the line of shadow came to an abrupt halt, metres away.

It took Danny a second to remember how to breathe again. He stood and looked at the tiny stoat as it lay on the ground, panting heavily. Its sleek body was dark brown, its neat bib a sparkling white.

Its eyes gleamed with hatred.

He couldn't believe it. The shadows had come from Tom – he'd been so sure of it. He'd journeyed and journeyed to find Tom, and suddenly, in a matter of minutes, the shadows had gone from being Tom's fault – Danny's fault – to this.

A tiny brown stoat.

How on earth had he got it so wrong?

'Who are you?' was all that Danny could think to ask.

The stoat didn't seem to be able to run away, but righted itself and crouched on the thin grass, staring up at him madly. 'I was Iaco.'

'You were? Who are you now?'

'Nobody!' shrieked the stoat, lunging forward to show off its bared teeth.

Danny shrank back, but held the book and pencil ready. 'Why did you bring the shadows over? I thought they were from a tormented soul . . .'

The stoat glared up at him. 'And so they were. Do you not think a stoat can feel torment?'

'You're the tormented soul?'

The stoat swallowed, and fixed its hard black eyes on his. 'I had a family once,' it said. 'All killed by men with dogs. All of them. Not in the honourable way that stoats kill, swiftly and for food. Just men and dogs, far greater in size than us, killing for the sake of hanging a few little bodies on fences and watching them rot in the sun.'

157

Bile rose in Danny's throat. 'But that's horrible,' he said. 'That's really sick.'

'That's humans!' spat the stoat. 'Don't pretend you wouldn't do it yourself. You are human. Humans are cruel. So I decided to kill as many humans as I could. Not in the swift merciful way that we stoats believe in, but in a slow, lingering, hopeless way. I did well. Very well.'

'But you can't have managed all that on your own. You must have been helped by somebody. Was it – ?'

'Somebody helped me!' The little stoat curled up its paw and waved it, cackling hysterically. 'Oh yes, of course! I could never have enough fury to destroy the world on my own. I was sent by Sammael, of course! An avenging angel! Of course!'

'Sammael! I knew it.' Heat surged in Danny's cheeks.

The stoat stopped waving its paw and glared at him. 'Did you miss the sarcasm? I did it myself, you blockhead. My fury is my own. For sure, I got the shadow from Sammael, back when he had some power – I only had to bite a piece off, each time I laid it, and the bitten piece grew into a new patch. A marvellous creation! But then Sammael's power shrivelled and died, while mine grew like the blossom in springtime. What a pity it had to end. No matter – I've spread my fury far and wide!'

Danny's rage ran hot through his blood, pushing into his skin and up to the surface. His whole body tingled. He ignored the stoat's words as the name of Sammael pounded through his head like the bouncing boulders of a rockfall. 'I knew it was Sammael! He's at the bottom of everything evil. I knew it!'

'Ha!' screamed Iaco. 'He told me about you – you are stupider than he said! We all have powers from Sammael. I spread shadows. Your horse and your friend follow his footsteps in Chromos. Your hare talks to humans. You –'

'I've got nothing from Sammael,' said Danny.

'Except your dog.'

Danny opened his mouth to deny it, and couldn't speak.

We all have powers from Sammael.

Ori had appeared out of nowhere, unasked for, and saved his life. He had accepted her willingly, and he hadn't questioned her loyalty.

Tom had done the same, when Sammael had offered him all the knowledge he wanted. He'd taken hold of the gift with two keen hands, and he hadn't looked at what lay behind it. And now Tom was dead, and never coming back.

Was Ori, too, an arrow from Sammael's bow?

Ori crept forward, closer to the stoat. Her lips were drawn back, her fluffy hackles risen. Her thick body crouched, ready to pounce.

The stoat turned its head and gave a peal of chattering laughter. 'You may kill me, dog. But you will only do it because I have chosen to die!'

Ori trembled, eyes narrowing, and growled low in the throat.

'Come on!' taunted the stoat. 'Come on! You've got me now! I've told him about you! Finish me off!'

'Wait!' said Danny. 'Ori, get back!'

The stoat sneered, and turned its back on Ori. 'Come and get me, dog!' it said. 'Come on! Get your revenge!'

'It's evil,' said Ori. 'That animal is evil. Don't listen to it.'

'I will,' said Danny. 'I want to hear what it's got to say.'

Could Ori understand what the stoat was saying?

Danny's mind seized up. It couldn't be true. Ori, his companion. His friend. His saviour, from out of the deep, deep blue.

Ori pounced.

Iaco the stoat was dead in a quick snap of jaws and shaking of head, the smooth brown back broken in two.

Ori threw the stoat's little body in the air and snapped at it as it came down. It fell on the ground and lay there, and the world was quiet.

'Ori . . .' was all Danny could say. He buzzed with a strange fury. How dare this stoat be dead? How dare it lie there, so sleek and brown, and not be able to tell him more, to gloat more, to look back at the land it had turned grey? How dare it be so small?

Ori stood defiantly.

She looked like the same dog. She was the same dog, of course.

He loved her.

But he hated Sammael.

'You were sent by Sammael,' said Danny, bleakly. 'Don't deny it.'

'He did send me,' said Ori. 'He sent me to help you to be brave.'

Danny shook his head. 'Sammael doesn't want me to be brave,' he said. 'He wants me to be dead. What did he tell you to do?'

'Just that,' insisted Ori. 'To give you strength and courage.'

'I don't believe you,' said Danny, turning from her. 'You're a liar.' He'd never understood how Cath had forgiven Barshin for lying to her, and he didn't understand it now.

Cath coughed behind them, and Danny turned. She was greyer than ever. The shadows were too close. He had to lift them.

'What happened?' Cath asked.

'It was the stoat. It got a patch of shadow from Sammael, and used it to call up the clouds. Look, there's one it dropped.' He pointed over to the place, a short distance away, where the black patch lay under the clouds, holding them huddled over the earth.

Cath glanced at the shadow, then at the little bundle of fur on the ground.

'That thing? It don't look much.'

Iaco's body was smaller than Barshin. Smaller than Cath's shoe, even. She could have crushed the stoat with a single stamping foot.

'Sammael doesn't look much,' said Danny. 'None of the things he comes up with do.'

Cath touched the toe of her trainer to the stoat's nose, then to the tip of its tail.

'So it wasn't nothing to do with Tom at all?'

Danny nodded. 'It was a soul in torment, but not Tom.'

Holding the pencil-point to the page, he pulled some words out of his still-churning brain.

'After Iaco was dead, all the small patches of shadow that the stoat had spread around the country disappeared.'

The shadow-patch began to fade.

'So what's Ori done?' Cath's question was sharp, and Danny's neck stung at the sound of the dog's name.

'Ori's from Sammael, too,' he said. The words were flat and hard and heavy.

Cath shrugged. 'He's not all bad, then, is he?'

Danny exploded. 'Of course he is!' he spat. 'They're all evil! Sammael! Iaco! Barshin! Ori! They've all betrayed us!'

Cath reached to touch the tips of Barshin's ears. 'But they've helped us too,' she said, quietly. 'You'd never have seen Chromos without Barshin. You'd never have escaped the shadows without Ori. You'd never have done anything at all without Sammael – you'd still be at home, sitting inside and asking Mummy and Daddy for permission to scratch your bum. Sammael made you get up and fight. What would you be if you didn't have nothing to fight?'

'I'd be safe,' said Danny. 'I'd be happy.'

'You'd be bored,' said Cath.

'So what?' He was sick of her taking Sammael's side. Trying to make him agree that danger and chaos was better than safety. 'I'm going to find Sammael and kill him. Are you coming?'

Cath stared at him. Barshin stared too, through narrower eyes.

'What about them shadows?' said Cath. 'Aren't you going to write them lifting?'

'They're going,' said Danny. 'I've made all the shadow patches disappear. When they've gone, the clouds will lift and scatter, then the sun will break through.'

'Yeah, the sun will come,' said Cath. 'But things didn't go grey from there being no sun, did they?'

'Yes they did,' said Danny.

'Idiot! The shadows blocked out Chromos, don't you get it? Only Chromos can make the colours come back. Sammael puts Chromos on Earth. Without him, everything will stay grey.'

'No it won't!' yelled Danny, his blood running hot with outrage. 'We don't need Sammael! If we need any more of Chromos on earth, I'll bring it here! I've got *The Book of Shadows*!'

'You don't get it, do you?' Cath rubbed her tired face. 'Sammael isn't trying to hurt everyone! He just does things, and that changes the world, all the time. Yeah, when you're happy, something comes along to make you sad. But it works the other way, too. And Sammael does both.'

Danny couldn't answer her. She'd got it wrong. So wrong. The only thing he could do was to kill Sammael, and then Cath would see. Why had he always thought that she was wise? She didn't know anything at all.

He turned away, turned his whole back on her, and looked down at the little book in his hand. For a moment, it seemed like a symbol of everything that had gone wrong in his life. The page in front of him was always blank, and it was always he who had to hold the pencil and work out what to write on it.

But I'm forgetting, he told himself, that I can build a whole new world with this book. Maybe I can't bring the past back, but I can write the future however I want it to be. I can make a boat to sail the high seas, and every time the waves get rough, I can write them calm again.

And it struck him that Cath knew that, too, and was probably jealous. Who wouldn't be jealous of him?

Well, let her be, he thought. I offered her a part in it, and she went off on one. I'll go and do the rest myself.

'Fine,' he said. 'I'm off. Come on, Shimny.'

The ghost horse threw up her head and backed away from him.

'Don't be silly,' said Danny. 'It's just me.'

The mare kept her head high and looked down at him along her nostrils, rolling her eye until it showed half white. 'I will not go into *The Book of Shadows*,' she said.

For a moment, Danny was tempted just to write his demands in the book. They'd all have to obey him. He opened it, pencil poised, and looked down at the page.

What was the point of wasting paper on stupid girls and hysterical horses? They could get lost. He had an enemy to fight.

'Fine,' he said to Shimny. 'You're all welcome to each other. Bunch of losers.'

He watched the scorn on Cath's face. She thought he was just weak. He'd show her.

'I don't want anything to do with any of you,' he said. 'I'm going to kill Sammael and make the world safe again.'

'The world ain't ever been safe,' said Cath.

'Well, then I'll make a new world!' shouted Danny. 'My own world! A much better one than this! And none of you will be in it!'

He turned away and stamped off along the hillside, so that he could quickly put distance between himself and them all before he was tempted to write something nasty happening to them in *The Book of Shadows*.

Behind him, Cath and Barshin looked at Ori. Ori, head down, nosed once at the little body of Iaco the stoat and trotted off after her master.

'What are we going to do?' asked Barshin, as Cath stared after Ori.

Cath, about to shrug, stopped herself. 'How is it he don't see that some things you're scared of are bad, and some are good?' she said, more to herself than Barshin. 'Ain't he happy about the things he's already done?'

'He's grieving for Tom,' said Barshin. 'Grief brings with it a whole army of pain, in all sorts of different liveries. Even if he could ever see how Sammael's changed him for the better, he wouldn't be able to right now.'

'But he's gone off to kill Sammael, not to get Tom back.'

'He can't get Tom back. He knows, deep down, that no one can change the past.'

Cath turned to the hare. 'We should help him see it then, shouldn't we? Let's get Tom and put him to rest, like Danny wanted to.'

'But we can't go to Chromos,' said Barshin. 'We're grey.'

'Then let's finish this,' said Cath. She unwrapped the bundle of rags that she'd been clutching for so long, and lay it on the muddy grass. It was a jumble of scraps of cloth of every colour under the sun – greens, greys, blues and browns, yellows and pinks and reds.

Barshin stared at it. 'I saw you making it,' he said. 'I saw it got its colour back, when you got most of yours, and I knew it must be something to do with your soul. But is it meant to have a pattern? A picture? I don't see –'

'It's my Chromos,' said Cath. 'The colours of me. That grey, that's the concrete of the Sawtry, and that pink, that's my stepmum's nail polish, and the green, there, my old schoolbag, and that white is Ida's house, and that grey, that's Ida's hair. Red, that's Johnny White's . . . loads more. Everything. I made it so I could wrap it around myself and try to get to Chromos on my own. I thought if I could make the outside of myself look like the inside, Chromos might take me in. If I didn't hide anything, just showed all the colours that I am, I might somehow . . . fit Chromos. Become a part of it.'

'Why didn't it work before, then?'

Cath smiled. 'It ain't finished, idiot,' she said. 'There's one more colour to get.'

Chapter 17

A Hole in the Sky

Danny scuffed his trainers on the muddy hillside grass. How should he kill Sammael?

Well, what had Sammael done to him? Tried to chop him in half with an axe. Chased him with a pack of dogs. Nearly drowned him, several times. Made him go mad. Nearly turned him grey and hopeless.

Any of those ways would have been a fitting end for Sammael, too. A storm would have been even better. He'd like to kill Sammael with a storm. Except – there was something a little too magical about storms. He had to be sure that Sammael really died, and wasn't just transported into another world, or blasted into an acorn and left to lie around the earth making mischief.

He went for practicality.

Picking up the book, he wrote '*Danny got a massive sword*'.

Three more steps along the tufty hillside, and he stumbled over it. A slender silver weapon, somewhat disappointingly thin, in a golden scabbard. In his hand, the blade was weightless as a beam of light. He swung it a couple of times, slashing through the air, watching the silver gleam, and then buckled the scabbard around his waist.

This hillside wasn't the place, though. He had to do it somewhere far away from Cath and the others. He couldn't have their disapproval tainting his triumph.

'*Danny went to a high mountaintop . . .*'

Quickly he crossed out '*mountain*' and wrote '*hill*'. The book was quite literal after all, and he wasn't dressed for snow.

He found himself standing on a hilltop, in the middle of country he didn't recognise at all. A wide green jungle rolled out on all sides below him. He was far from home, and he hadn't written Ori's name in the book . . . but she was at his feet, looking up at him.

'Go away,' he said. 'I don't want you here.'

'You're my master,' said Ori. 'I can't leave you, whatever madness you fall into.'

Danny turned away from her. I'm alone against the world, he thought. Everyone thinks I've gone mad. But I'm right. I know I am.

Without warning, the sky in front of him split from top to bottom, and a huge tear opened up in the daylight. Inside its jagged edges he saw darkness. The clear air sagged aside in gossamer curtains, and the blackness beckoned.

He looked down at the book – had he just written something without realising it? Had he made a mark like a rip on the page?

The page was half full, but the words ended at '*Danny went to a high hilltop . . .*'

Danny tore the sky in two?

From inside the blackness, a whispering began. At first it sounded only like the wind through trees, but gradually it rose to a wail, then to a shriek, and then it began to move.

It shuddered.

It shook.

It trembled, harder and harder, until Danny knew that something was about to erupt from it and come screaming out towards him. Frantically, he wrote, '*The hole in the sky closed up*'.

The hole in the sky closed up.

And opened again.

The trembling grew worse. Deep inside the blackness, faces gathered. Their mouths were open, each one stretching to wail out a sound that lay between the howl of the wind and the cry of a lost wolf. Hair streamed around their faces and their eyes were empty and lightless, and they were looking at him, every single one of them.

As the darkness swelled and bulged, he realised they were fighting each other, scrambling towards the hole, and their mouths were opening and closing, taking bits of something from the air around them.

The daylight. They were eating the daylight.

Already the air around the hole was darker. Darkness was easily dealt with – Danny narrowed his eyes and thought of Chromos and expected to see colour breaking through. But this darkness held no colour. The more he looked into it, the colder his skin became, and the colder the hand that held the pencil, frozen, on the open page of *The Book of Shadows*. And then he knew.

They were eating the daylight, but what lay underneath it wasn't darkness.

It was shadow.

His fingers twitched. He had to stop them before they reached him. What should he call them? Banshees? Spectres? Zombies?

He began to write – fast and hurried, not bothering to keep his writing small, using up line after line in his haste.

'*The colours came back – they leapt into Danny's hand – his sword was made of colours, and every time he swung it, the air was full of colour, and it dissolved the shadows . . .*'

He raised the sword into the air and swung it back and forth, waiting for a trail of colours to fly in its wake. But the sword was gleaming, cold and silver, and although its blade was pure and sharp, it left nothing except a glint of light as it sliced through the air.

Danny pushed the sword back into the scabbard. The wailing faces were bursting through the hole, now, tumbling over each other in their desperate haste. The air was grimy with shadow. As Danny breathed, it choked his nose and dried his throat.

He wrote, frantically. '*Danny was in control. He pushed the shadows away. He pushed them with his hands – the world was fine – everything was fine – Danny beat the shadows – he could do anything –*'

'Nice try.'

A figure stepped through the shadows, straight from the air in front of Danny. Curly-haired and thin, he wore a torn shirt and the bare soles of his feet struck hard against the red earth of the hilltop.

Danny looked up into the coal-black eyes. Finally, they were together.

This was how it would end, then – he had written that he, Danny, was as powerful as anything could ever be.

And in answer, Sammael had come.

Sammael pushed aside the faces as if they were the branches of a weeping willow. They recoiled from his hands and settled down behind him, simmering.

It's because he's got Chromos on him, thought Danny, desperately. If only I had written that I had Chromos on me, they wouldn't have been able to touch me –

'Honestly,' said Sammael. 'Can't you do better than that? That book is another world! Can't you fight a few moaning faces with it?'

The faces jostled and lunged up towards Danny. Sammael batted them lazily backwards, and again they shrank away.

'I'm not scared of the faces,' said Danny, gripping the hilt of his silver sword defiantly. 'As soon as I can think of the right words, I can beat them. I can do anything.'

He found that his face had twisted into a tight smile.

Sammael threw back his head and laughed. The faces leapt in fright, and a gleam of sunshine caught his black curls. When his eyes came back to Danny again, his cheeks were shining.

'You think you can kill me?'

'Yeah.'

'Do you even know what I am?'

'You're dead,' said Danny.

'If you say so,' said Sammael. 'You really want me dead?'

Danny didn't have to hesitate. 'Yes!' he said, gripping the sword and *The Book of Shadows*. 'It's what everyone wants! Without you, there'll be no more bad dreams. No more huge storms, or people going mad, or suffocating in the shadows. We can just live how we want.'

'But without dreams,' said Sammael.

'So what? We don't need dreams. We'll just go to sleep, and wake up safe in the morning. It'll be amazing.'

Sammael looked at him quietly, and for a second Danny saw it again – the way that face could look evil or kind, terrible or soft, how it could remind him of his worst enemy and his best friend.

He forced his eyes away, refusing to be drawn in. He knew what he was looking at, now. Those grey streets – that fearful sky – this was the fount of all of it.

Danny adjusted his grip on the pen. '*Then Danny killed Sammael with the sword,*' he wrote.

Carefully, he put the book down on the red earth and took the sword in both hands, raising it above his head. Closing his eyes, he swung downwards.

When he opened his eyes, Sammael was still standing close to him, exactly where he had swung the blade.

Sammael shrugged. 'We're still on Earth,' he said. 'I am of no earth.'

'Fine,' said Danny. 'How about this, then?'

He took a new page in the book.

'*Suddenly, Danny discovered that his sword was made of a magic metal. It was the one metal in the universe that could kill anything. It could chop Sammael into tiny little pieces that could never be put back together again. Sammael had no idea that any metal like that existed . . .*' He looked up at Sammael, who was watching him write, and felt the tight little smile tighten further. '*But it was a new metal that had just been invented, and nobody had any way to defend themselves against it. Not weapons. Not legends. Not words. This was the deadliest thing in the whole universe, and Danny's sword was made of it.*'

Carefully, he put *The Book of Shadows* and the pencil back into his pocket, and then he picked up the newly magical sword.

Sammael stood in front of him, framed by the shadow faces. As Danny looked at them, their mouths opened again and more sound came out. Not wailing, this time. A high, soft keening, that wandered across the air and tumbled up to the clouds. There was music in it, and there was sorrow, and regret.

The faces still pushed and shoved around Sammael, but they never got too close; they left a wide space around him, free from shadow, as they strained forwards. They'll leave no space around me, thought Danny. Once he's gone, they'll try to eat me alive. But I'll stop them.

And for a second he looked at Sammael and saw him framed with the last light left in that part of the sky, and he saw that the light was clinging to Sammael, pressing itself close to him in an attempt to escape the devouring shadows. The light was seeking refuge in Sammael, and he was standing there in his filthy clothes, with his battered, ancient face full of scorn, and he was shining as brightly as a lantern in a vast, midnight forest.

It was a trick. It was all a trick designed to throw Danny off his purpose. But the time for Sammael's tricks had come and gone.

Danny kept his eyes open, and swung the sword.

The magical metal flashed.

Sammael's broken corpse lies on the red earth.

After all that horror, it is over. Danny stands and leans on his sword. The world is free of Sammael, and he is the one who has freed it. If only he had done this long ago, Tom might still be alive –

But there is nothing to be gained from thinking that now. Sammael is dead at last. At least Danny thought of the right words, wrote them down, and finally made it happen.

He remembers, in that distant time before his ears were singing with blood and his arms were shaking with relief and his stomach was churning with bile, that there were other creatures in this, too.

A horse. A girl. A hare. A dog.

All of his friends, when he saw them last, were suffering. He can put that right.

He writes in the book – words he can't quite keep track of as they rush from his pencil – something about a horse and Death and a home. The horse will be all right. He has seen to that.

As for the others –

It is time to build a new world.

This time, he watches himself write, and the words are small and purposeful, and the letters are precise.

'Danny makes the world again, from the beginning.'

Chapter 18

Home

Cath kept close to the walls. She never felt safe in this town. Once, she had hoped that she might never have to see it again, but hope was a vain thing. Overhead, the shadows had gone. The sky was clear and pale, and winter had crept back timidly into the air; an edge of sharpness scratched around Cath's cheeks and nipped Barshin's ears.

On the ground, everything was still grey.

'Is this necessary?' asked Barshin. 'You hate this place.'

'I told you, I know what I need,' snapped Cath.

'And I hate this place.'

'Makes two of us, then.'

'And we're being followed by that – creature.' Barshin shuddered, risking a glance over his shoulder at Shimny. The ghost horse was plodding blindly along behind them, nose to the pavement, knees sagging. 'Why is she still following us?'

'You was fine with her when we needed her,' Cath pointed out.

'She's dead,' said Barshin. 'I don't like dead things. They're unnatural.'

Cath squinted back at Shimny, pale and lumbering, faded eyes blank. It was easy to see Barshin's point of view. The horse didn't exactly make your heart glad.

'I reckon we'll need her again,' said Cath. 'And she's not doing any harm. Nobody else notices her.'

Cath was right. The people who walked past them had their heads down, eyes fixed to the ground. Their skins were still grey from their time under shadows, and although they weren't aimless any more, none of them looked interested in wherever they were going.

'I can't believe I used to live here,' said Cath. 'It's grim.'

'It wasn't like that, then,' Barshin reminded her. 'It hadn't been shadowed.'

'The Sawtry didn't need no shadows. It had its own.'

When she said the word Sawtry, a cold hand poked its fingers into her belly and twisted them about. She hadn't forgotten the estate while she'd been living in Ida's house, but she'd managed to convince herself that she would never have to go back there.

The wide spaces of the beach. The grass-covered dunes. The foothills. The fields. The forests.

Cath's heart bled dark crimson into her chest. She clutched at the bundle of rags slung over her shoulder. Spring green. Turquoise and primrose yellow, and the purple of heather on a heath. Greys, light and strong. Browns, bright and dark. A hundred shades of green, from yellow to ochre to brilliant jade. She had caught them all, mashed up plants, mixed in dirt and berries and the dark juices of tree sap, and dyed any fragment of unused material she could find. And the cloak was almost finished. Almost.

The sky flickered.

Barshin glanced upwards. 'What's he doing?'

The sky flickered again.

'Maybe it's just a storm coming?' suggested Cath. 'Bound to be something strange happening, what with all them clouds on the move.'

'I don't like it,' said Barshin. 'I think we'd better hurry.'

'He won't write anything about us,' said Cath. 'He wouldn't dare. We'll be safe.'

Barshin looked at her, his ears twitching. There was a gold light in his eyes, which couldn't have been the reflection of the lifeless sun. Then the sky flickered again, and this time the flickering was red. There was no mistaking it for lightning.

'He is grieving,' said Barshin. 'He has lost a person he loves. It is a very simple thing, and it breaks your world, so that you must build it anew. My guess is that he's going to write a new world, and destroy this one.'

The sky gave a groan, and there was the gold again in Barshin's eyes, and when Cath looked up she saw that the sun was directly above them. It had taken on the size and colour of a late evening sun, blazing and orange, and it was sinking in the sky, not towards the horizon but straight downwards, growing slowly larger.

The ground should have been bright with sunshine. But the ground was grey. People were still grey. Nobody looked up.

'Can they see it?' Cath pointed upwards, aware of the warmth on the top of her head.

'No.' Barshin hovered for a moment on his haunches, front paws dangling in the air. 'They're not looking for it. They won't see it. They won't know anything, till it's all over.'

'How long have we got?' Cath cast a desperate look about her. They'd left the market square behind, but she could still see Shimny in the middle of it, dolefully sniffing at the fountain.

Barshin shook his head. 'I don't know,' he said. 'A few hours?'

'Shimny!' Cath yelled across the echoing market square. 'Shimny, come on!'

The horse lifted its head, ears pricked for a second.

The sky flashed scarlet.

This time, Shimny saw, too. As the sky cracked, all the patches of her coat that had once been black flooded with a red that shone as bright as blood. She tossed her head and snorted, taking a step or two backwards. Her white patches turned gold.

'Shimny!' Cath yelled again.

The horse reared up on her hind legs and came galloping towards them, red and gold coat gleaming in the growing strength of the sun. As she reached Cath, the girl was afraid for a second to touch her, sure that the scarlet patches would hold the fierce heat of flames.

But Cath was made of fire, wasn't she? Nothing could burn her.

She reached for the horse's mane and found it cool under her fingertips. Cooler than life could be – despite the colour, the horse was still dead. But that didn't seem to matter now.

Cath scrambled up onto the broad gold back and reached down for Barshin. The hare leapt into her arms. For a second, the old feeling of being astride Zadoc ran through Cath's blood so strongly that she was certain the world would vanish the moment they started moving. But as she kicked Shimny's sides, the ground stayed hard and grey beneath them, and the buildings stretched hard and grey on both sides, and Shimny was the only colour in all of it – a great shining streak of red and gold, leaping down the bare streets.

Cath gasped and let go of Barshin to grab at Shimny's mane with both hands as the ghost sailed over a fallen lamppost. Barshin clung to Cath, cramming his huge hindlegs down into the waistband of her jeans.

Ahead, deserted cars were strewn about the road, and Shimny ran towards them, caught by the brilliance of the sky, her tail a stream of gold fire. Cath tugged desperately, trying to hold her back, to slow her, but the horse plunged on, soaring over bonnets and doors. Cath closed her eyes for a second and then forced them open, angry at herself. What was this? Fear? She wasn't afraid of anything. Cath Carrera didn't believe in fear.

Shimny kicked on. Cath began to drum her heels on the horse's sides, pulling her mane to steer her. What was the answer if you were afraid of going fast?

Go faster.

The sky above them darkened as the flashes came faster. They dived under a bridge.

Flash.

The tunnel lit up crimson and purple. The sun glowed orange, turning to red. Nearly there now. Nearly there.

They raced over the main road, normally choked with speeding cars and lorries. Nobody was bothering to drive today. Nobody was going fast.

And on the other side – the Sawtry, tower blocks clambering into the sky. The concrete yards and playgrounds spread beneath Shimny's hooves. There was Cath's old block, doors standing open. Cath yanked Shimny's head around and pointed her towards the stairs.

The ghost horse made nothing of stairs. Cath slid backwards onto her rump and held on for all her life with both hands twisted around thick bunches of mane. Outside, the sky growled and spat. The light coming in through the scratched panes of window glass was a burning orange, as bright as if a fire had been lit just outside. But the only fire that could be burning up here was the sun.

Cath urged Shimny up the stairs and to the end of the corridor. The last door on the left, next to another glowing window. The light in the corridor flashed, orange, red, purple – and just once, a white as bright and blinding as the world without shadows had been.

Outside the door, Cath swung her leg over Shimny's back and slid to the ground. She didn't want to go inside the flat. Every nerve in her body screamed against it – bubbles rose in her stomach until she felt so sick that she could barely think. But there was nothing out here that was going to help her.

She nearly raised her hand to the door, to knock on it. But what was she thinking? If anyone was there, they would hardly just hand over what she wanted.

They would grab her.

They would take her into the living room.

They would use the dogs to guard her.

They would get Dad.

And she had promised herself that she would never have to face him again. That was the kind of promise you had to keep, if you wanted your life to be worth anything at all.

So she leant back, raised her leg, and threw herself against the door, trying to kick it open.

She was shoved out of the way by a round, soft bulk that shone scarlet and gold as it slammed against the grey-green door. Shimny's square old rump, thudding backwards.

'Thanks, old lady,' grinned Cath, as the door buckled and splintered, falling inwards over the piles of rubbish that always littered the hallway of the flat.

And Dad came roaring out of the living room, with a baseball bat.

Cath stared, for one terrible second, as Dad raised the bat high and swung it at Shimny. She braced herself for the impact, ready for Shimny to stagger and fall to the ground.

The bat glanced off Shimny's solid neck. The horse stood still, unflinching.

Cath's heart leapt. Of course! He couldn't hurt a ghost! He could only hurt living things.

Like her and Barshin.

Dad swung the bat around and stood, facing her.

Cath watched the bat for a second. It was shaking slightly. Dad had lost weight. He had always been big and solid: he filled a room whenever he walked into it, and took all the light that was trying to filter through to the smaller people. But there was less of him now. She could see past him to the living room door.

The flat was very quiet. No TV. No dogs, either. They were always the first to rush to the door.

'Don't you move,' Dad said. 'Don't you move a finger.'

'Or what?' said Cath.

The bat went very still. Dad wasn't shaking any more. The cold was coming over his silvery blue eyes and he was forgetting who she was. It always happened to him before he went wild.

Cath squared her chin. So this was it. She was shrouded in all the colours of Chromos, except one. So close to the end, so close to stepping out of the world in one direction, and Dad was going to hold her here, and she would step out of it in a completely different direction altogether.

It wasn't fair, she thought.

But then not much had ever been fair, and she hadn't minded before. Why should she mind now?

It was quite funny, if you thought about it. Everything had gone mad. Danny had gone maddest of all. The whole world was about to burn up, as soon as he figured out what insanity to write into *The Book of Shadows*. Cath regretted that she wouldn't find out what it was, but it didn't matter much. Danny's world was never going to be the kind of world she wanted. She wanted Chromos, or nothing.

Looks like it's nothing, eh? She grinned to herself.

And then Barshin moved.

She'd forgotten the power he had, to leap and kick and fly through the air. He sprang from her arms and hurled himself against Dad, and Dad threw up his arms to defend himself. The bat fell. Shimny's rump went crashing into the hallway, sending Dad staggering backwards, pinning him to the wall, squashing his chest. She might be a ghost, but she seemed solid enough when it counted.

Cath didn't hesitate. She squeezed herself between the horse's cold flank and the wall until she was in the living room doorway.

She'd never had a bedroom of her own when she'd lived here. She'd slept on the settee in this living room, and hidden anything precious in her locker at school. Anything precious would have disappeared as soon as Dad's other kids got their hands on it.

This thing wasn't precious. It was silly to be sentimental over stuff that meant nothing in itself, and it was even more stupid to be sentimental about things that had been left behind by mothers who'd abandoned you when you were a baby. Cath hardly remembered her mum at all.

'She was wild,' was all Dad had ever said.

'She didn't want you,' his girlfriend Macy had added, plenty of times.

Cath went to the far corner of the room, behind the TV, and peeled back a corner of the carpet, fishing underneath it and pulling out a short length of emerald green ribbon. She had found it one day, when she'd been about five. Back then, she'd dreamed about her mum most nights, and in every dream her mum had worn an emerald green dress. She'd realised that the dress must have been real, and the ribbon must have belonged to her mum.

It wasn't precious. She'd left it under the carpet. So what if one of the other kids found it? But none of them ever had.

She curled her fingers securely around the ribbon and ran back into the hallway.

'Come on!' she said to Barshin, leaping up onto Shimny's red and gold back.

And something in her couldn't resist turning back to Dad, squashed against the wall, and waving the green ribbon in his face.

'Remember?' she said. 'Remember?'

Dad's face was baffled. 'What?'

'Remember *her*?'

'Macy?'

'Mum. *My* mum.'

He frowned, and then his face spread into a grin, understanding and sly.

'*That*? That's off one of Macy's tops. Used to wear it all the time, years back. You was too young to remember, I reckon.'

Cath looked at the ribbon, momentarily uncertain. But then she knew.

'Who cares? My mum was wild! And I'm wild!'

She kicked at Shimny's flanks and the fiery ghost shot forwards, back over the ruined door and out into the hallway. Cath clutched the green ribbon and the bundled-up Chromos cloak, and held the world in her hands. The cloak was the colour of all that she was, and the emerald green was the colour of the last and most hidden part of her. So what if it wasn't the colour of her missing mother? It was the colour of a strong and powerful hope that belonged entirely to her.

She clattered down the corridor and down the stairs, knowing for absolute certain that this was the last, last, last time she would ever go down them, that her feet would never come this way again. It was over – completely over. This part of her life was gone, and she had escaped it.

Outside, she looked for the last time around the yard. It wasn't grey any more – the sun was spreading to fill the sky, and the concrete had cracked into a dried-up riverbed. The sky was flashing every second now – yellow, crimson, purple, black –

Cath flung the cloak over her head, blocking out the rays of the fierce sun. It was a thick cloak, but the light still found its way through some of the holes. To Cath, underneath it, the cloak began to blaze in a tapestry of colour.

It was a stained-glass window. Only instead of a dozen or so colours, it had a hundred, and she was standing on one side of it, looking out at the burning world through all the shades of her own heart.

There were the greens of joy. The blues of wonder. The browns of stubbornness and determination. The reds of fear and hope. The purples of scorn and bravery. The yellows of frustration and excitement. They were all there – everything that lay inside her, pushing her feet forward. They were all there, except one.

And there was a space between pale yellow and pale green – a small gap and a loop of blue string.

She pushed the ribbon through the hole, tying it into a knot, and the cloak was complete.

The colours mixed together, falling on her. She had made a window that showed exactly what it was like to be Cath Carrera. Probably nobody but herself could ever really understand it, but that didn't matter. She understood it.

And Chromos would understand.

'I can't tell you to go to Chromos,' shouted Cath to Shimny, as she wrapped the cloak around herself and Barshin, draping it over the horse's flanks. 'You can't understand me. But you know stuff, don't you? You know what needs to happen!'

And she drummed her heels into the flanks of the red and gold ghost, urging Shimny forward. Dry shrubs, drained of their sap, began to catch fire around them. Under the cloak, Cath heard the crackle of flames and felt the powerful kick of the horse as Shimny leapt into top speed. When she looked down at the ground beside Shimny's shoulder, Cath saw that they were galloping over flames, and that Shimny's hooves weren't beating so hard against the concrete. They were melting away, as Zadoc's hooves had once done, and they were dissolving into an air that was clear and cool, gentle as it rolled over a vast expanse of green grass and coloured flowers and wandering animals of every kind.

Shimny was running into Chromos, with Cath and Barshin on her back. Cath was guiding them, and Chromos was no longer grey.

'Don't stop,' urged Barshin. 'Don't slow down. Take us through it, all the way to the aether. There's no time to waste any more.'

'She can't go to the aether, can she? We'll have to stop and work out another way.'

'She couldn't go before, but look at her now, red and gold – she's a horse of fire! Something's changed her – I bet she can get there now. Try it!'

Cath flung back the cloak, so that it hung over her shoulders and draped itself over Shimny's rump. She gazed around at the great plain as they swept over it, Shimny's head thrusting forward to the rhythm of her gallop.

Chromos was paradise. Why should they go to the aether, just to try to put things right for Danny? The aether was white and airless. Cath never wanted to go back to Earth anyway – what did it matter what happened to it?

Cath tugged at the horse's gold mane. Shimny's pace slackened to a gentle canter.

'I'm not going!' Cath said, as the detail of Chromos began springing to life around her. 'I'm staying here. You can try getting her to go up to the aether and you can sort things out if you want – I don't care about the world any more!'

And she went to swing her leg off Shimny, to slide down to the ground.

'What are you doing?' squeaked Barshin. 'You can't get down!'

'I've got the cloak. I'll be safe. I belong here now.'

'No!' Barshin wriggled frantically against her belly, as if trying to push her back onto the horse. 'You need to come to the aether! You need to help me!'

'I said, I don't care about the world,' said Cath. 'I'm never going back. I'll live here!'

'But I can't live here!' Barshin pushed his face into her armpit.

'Yeah, you can. As long as you're under the cloak, you'll be fine.'

'I don't want to!' hissed the hare, his face creeping up towards Cath's ear. 'I am earth, remember? If you make me stay here, I'll die. If you let Earth be killed, you'll kill me.'

'Just imagine your own Earth,' tried Cath. 'It'll be here, exactly as you want it.'

'I want the Earth I can't imagine,' said Barshin. 'I want the real Earth, full of things I don't know and haven't had time to dream of yet. Let me have it.'

'You sort it out then,' said Cath. 'I'll leave you on Shimny. You do it, if that's what you want.'

She pulled the hare away from her. He screwed up his eyes and covered them with his forepaws.

'Please,' he said, so quietly that Cath couldn't tell if he was actually speaking, or if she was just putting words into his mouth. 'Please, if you have any heart left at all, help me.'

Cath's chest tightened. Of course she had a heart. But it was her heart, to keep her alive and protect her. Barshin was her friend, but if she cared for him, he would only betray her and hurt her. He'd betrayed her already, in fact.

Barshin dangled in the air, blind and helpless.

For a terrifying moment, she wanted to drop him. Then she would be alone, free to live in Chromos without any small voices suggesting it wasn't the right thing to do.

Chromos boiled. The land rose up under her feet into hills and mountains, pushing Cath, Shimny and Barshin high into the sky. Cracks ran through the earth as it dried. Shimny snorted and stepped sideways, and suddenly they were standing on the edge of a black abyss. Far below in the distant depths, molten lava steamed and bubbled.

If she dropped Barshin, now . . .

The lava rose in a single, surging wave. It reached out to Shimny's hooves, to Cath's feet, and Chromos was hotter than the burning earth, and Cath's skin was screaming.

And she knew where she had to go.

She kicked Shimny as the lava reached the golden hooves. The horse reared, spinning around on her hindlegs and leaping up into the air. Instead of sinking back down onto the floor of Chromos, her hooves found purchase on the currents of wind, and Cath tucked Barshin against her chest and held onto the horse's mane. The hare was right. Shimny had changed. She would run with them all the way up to the stars, if needed.

Barshin was warm, alive and trembling. His pulse was much faster than Cath's own, but for a single beat, their hearts pounded together.

Cath felt the hare falling. She gripped him with a savage anger that stopped a millimetre short of squeezing his life to a standstill, and knew that parting from Barshin was impossible now. She would never escape him. She would never be alone again, until the day that one or other of them died.

For a second, she felt Barshin's terrible blunt claws digging into her chest – right into her heart.

And then she kicked Shimny on, and the red and gold horse galloped into the sky.

Chapter 19

The Battle

The desert was wide and bare. As Danny stood facing it, he felt good.

Taller. Stronger. More certain.

The air was clean and new, with the dampness that comes after a summer rainstorm. The sun's rays warmed the sand, colouring it a gentle rust-brown. This was a desert now, but everything was about to grow.

For a second, he closed his eyes, imagining it. He'd build cities, oceans, deep dark forests and towering mountains. He'd make new animals and birds and fish. He'd pull in the tides, make rivers to sail down and lakes to swim in. He'd bring all the people from the old Earth, except for a few, perhaps. No Paul. Only a few of the teachers. No one from the Sawtry estate. But good people should come. *The Book of Shadows* would understand what Danny meant by 'good'. And he'd be sure to be specific about the ones he really didn't want, just in case it had any doubts.

The desert was quiet, waiting for his command. What should he begin with? Water? Mountains? Did he want it to look much like the old Earth, or could he change it all around a bit? Have some new places to explore, some uncharted territories? Yes, he liked the idea of that. He could spend his life being an explorer, like Shackleton or Scott, and show the world how brave he really was. He gripped the pencil and tried to think of how he might phrase it, preparing himself to open his eyes and write.

The sand trembled beneath his feet.

An earthquake? Surely nothing was supposed to happen that he hadn't written down?

The ground shook again.

And again.

Danny opened his eyes.

On the horizon, a black mass was spreading slowly towards him. The trembling was the sound of marching feet.

An army.

He looked down at the book. He'd written nothing about an army. This couldn't be happening. This was supposed to be his world, and nothing was supposed to happen in it that he hadn't dictated. For a second, he felt irritated. And then irritation gave way to fear, and fear gripped his chest.

Whose army was it?

Thud.

Thud.

Thud.

The army advanced across the wide plain. As they grew closer, Danny could see no colour about them at all. To a solider, they were black from head to foot. No – not black.

Clothed in shadows.

Their weapons were all different – pikes, swords, longbows, guns, cutlasses and daggers, knives and slingshots. They were a hundred different types of creature – men and women, lions and snakes, otters and bears and eagles in the sky. As they came closer, Danny saw smaller animals around the feet of the larger ones – ferrets and polecats, shrews and mice. There were many he didn't know the names of at all – rat-like creatures with huge ears that bounced along, lumbering squirrels the size of large dogs, stripy cats with fangs bigger than his arm that curled from their mouths in wicked arcs. Countless creatures, as far as his eyes could see, clothed in their blanket of black shadow, marching grimly towards him.

But he still had *The Book of Shadows*. He had the ultimate power. He could write them away in a word or two, as easy as that. There was nothing to fear.

Danny watched them come. No need to panic, just be ready to write. He wanted to see who they were, now that his heart had begun to slow again. He wanted to know who they had come from, so that he could be sure to eradicate it fully from his world.

He wrote in the book: '*The army stopped*'.

The army stopped.

He wrote: '*Their leader came forward*'.

A murmuring went up around the shadowed ranks; a rustling and clanking of steel swords and wooden spears.

The army parted, and a dark figure came slipping from between the ranks, his white shirt ghostly against the shadows.

He stood before Danny, the tight black curls of his hair shining beneath the sun. His face was the face of a thousand people Danny had known and would one day come to know. His expression was dignified and dangerous. His eyes were as black as midnight, and his cheeks were hollow and thin.

'But . . . you're dead,' said Danny.

Sammael inclined his head. 'I'm not sure that's entirely correct,' he said.

'I killed you. I wrote it into *The Book of Shadows*. You can't be here any more.'

'I go where I please,' said Sammael.

'No . . . This is the world of Mab! I rule everything! You're dead!'

'The world of Mab? What did you make it out of?'

Danny felt his cheeks redden. Sammael would only laugh at the truth. A handful of silly stories.

But what did it matter if Sammael laughed? Even if he'd escaped this time through some minor glitch, Danny would find out what it was and make sure it didn't happen again.

'The four elements,' he said defiantly. 'Earth, air, fire and water. It wasn't hard.'

'Only four?'

'There are only four. They're not the real elements, they're classical ones.'

'Ah,' said Sammael. 'I know the elements to which you refer, but I'm sorry to tell you, you've been misinformed. There's a fifth one.'

'You're lying.' Danny gripped the pencil stub and went to write again in the book. Then he looked up at Sammael, who smiled thinly.

'Ever heard of the aether?' said Sammael. 'The uppermost air. Only it isn't really air, is it? If you had to describe it, you might say it was . . . intangible. But nevertheless, aether is the fifth element. And I am aether.'

Danny stared at him, gripping the pencil and book.

'A world always has to hold something to surprise you,' said Sammael softly. 'Otherwise what kind of place would it be? You'd die of boredom in days.'

'I wouldn't,' said Danny. 'I'm going to make a world where everyone's happy, and everyone's safe. And there'll be no aether in it.'

'Of course there won't be,' said Sammael. 'The aether is the bit that contains imagination, which is terrifying and dangerous and wonderful. I was right about you. You're the last person in the world who should be let loose with a taro. Think of all that you could have done with it – and all you want is to use it to build a world without magic.'

'I'm using it for *good*!' snarled Danny. 'You're the one who does bad things, and doesn't care who gets hurt. You've been trying to destroy the whole world, with storms or Chromos or shadows. That's not great, is it?'

'Well,' Sammael put his head on one side, and for a moment his face was light. 'We all get cross when we're tired.'

'Tired!' Danny spat. 'You did all that, just because you were tired? And I'm wrong to want a world without you?'

'Yes,' said Sammael. 'Because a world without me would lose its wildness. And wildness is the life of the world! It is chaos; it is the unknown: it keeps the hearts of you mortal creatures singing out for the future. Without wildness, *your* world is this lifeless desert, waiting for your direction. And whatever world you build, even you, in time, will run out of ideas and become hopeless, and your world will be as brown and barren as you yourself are. Because you are only human, and wildness is a greater force than you will ever be.

'We can do without your kind of wildness, thanks very much,' said Danny. 'It's just spreading fear and danger. It doesn't matter to you – you'll never die, or have to see people you care about die. Though there was your dog, wasn't there? Kalia would still be alive, if you'd left me alone. So you even hurt yourself, with all this stuff. It didn't work very well, did it?'

'But that, my friend, is what life is for,' said Sammael, shrugging with a tightness that seemed to be holding the name of his dog away from his body. 'To feel *everything*. Joy *and* pain. Safety *and* terror. Gain. And loss. You can't select the ones you want, and try to keep the others from you. You can't panic as soon as the steering wheel slips out of your hands. If you seek to control everything, you are asking to live in fear of the moment when you lose control. And it will happen. It *does* happen.'

'It *won't* happen!' shouted Danny. 'I have *The Book of Shadows*! It'll never happen to me, never again!'

'It isn't always bad to lose control, you know,' said Sammael. 'Why don't you ask any of this lot?' He swept his arm around his vast, waiting army.

Danny glanced over the shadowed ranks. 'Who are they?'

'All my friends,' said Sammael. 'They are all the creatures who gave up their sand to me, so that I could continue to scatter Chromos about the Earth. In return, I opened their eyes to the world around them, in whichever ways they wanted. And they were so pleased with what they got, that all that remains of them will fight alongside me to beat you, and make sure I stay in the world.'

'But you can't beat me with an army!' laughed Danny. 'I can just write you to lose!' He let the sword rest in its scabbard and picked up the pencil. 'The pen is mightier than the sword!' he yelled, taunting. He'd heard it somewhere. It sounded good.

'*And Sammael's army vanished,*' he wrote.

The ranks of shadows advanced. They shouldered their weapons then raised them, beginning a chant that hissed around their ranks and stuttered out towards Danny.

'Chromos! Chromos! Chromos!'

'What's that?' said Sammael in his clear, cutting voice. 'You think they're *my* army? Think again!'

'*The Chromos army vanished,*' wrote Danny.

The weapons waved high in the air, and the ranks stayed. Not the Chromos army, then.

He was alone. There were thousands of them. He had no army.

'*The army in front of Danny vanished, whoever it belonged to. Danny had his own army. A bigger one. A very big bigger one. His own army –*' he began to scribble frantically.

Why wouldn't they vanish?

'*Danny knew why the army wouldn't vanish.*'

But the air was loud with the cries of thousands of shadows, and the book was silent. It seemed to have no knowledge to give him.

'*Danny's army could kill shadows –*'

They sprang up behind Danny, ranks and ranks of them – warlords with fur hats and machine guns; soldiers in tight red jackets mounted on cavalry horses; warriors stripped to the waist holding curving scythes; creaking tanks; nimble chariots pulled by shaggy ponies. Every kind of soldier was there, gathering round.

'Charge!' Danny yelled, dropping the book and fumbling for his sword.

No! He couldn't fight with them. He had to write all the right things, or he would lose. He saw Ori leaping into the fray, her golden coat shining in the stark desert sunlight. That traitor. Was she going to join Sammael's shadows?

No, she was attacking them. Fighting for him.

The shadows began to fall under the onslaught of Danny's fighters. Their darkness began to thin – he could almost see the sunlight behind them, now. He looked for Sammmael, wanting to see his defeated face.

Sammael was smiling.

He shouted something across to Danny, and pointed a hand across at a fallen swathe of shadows, and Danny watched in horror as the shadows began to glow. Yellow – no, green – no, orange – no, blue –

All the colours of the rainbow. All the colours of Chromos. All the colours of the vast universe.

'Dreams!' yelled Sammael, grinning broadly. 'They're not even an army! They're just dreams!'

Danny scribbled in the book. *'Danny's army killed dreams.'*

And his heart grew cold and leaden, and he dropped to his knees, trying to bear the terrible weight of it.

What did he want?

'Danny's army won. They fought the dreams, only just the dreams that Sammael controlled or the dreams that were anything to do with Sammael –'

Nothing changed. His heart grew heavier still. All dreams, gone . . .

Were all dreams to do with Sammael?

All of them?

'Danny kept his own dreams, the good ones, because he was going to make a new world even though there wasn't any point it would just be the same as the old one –'

He struggled to keep his pen straight, to remember what he had been trying to write.

'Danny's new world was going to be safe so that nothing could ever go wrong, so he had to win the fight –'

There was only space for one more line on the page. He tried to explain it all, exactly and precisely, trying to peer through the darkness in his mind.

'Danny beat Sammael, but saved the dreams.'

It was too vague. How, exactly?

'Danny's army killed –'

Not dreams. But who else?

No more room on the page. He turned it over.

200

'*Herbs to Cure Sore Hands.*'

He stared at the page.

The last page of the book. Already written on.

No space left.

If he could rub out some of the words –

But he didn't have anything to rub them out with.

The last page had got him, again.

He sank to his knees, and his warriors surged over him.

Chapter 20

The Book of Sand

Danny twisted away, trying to scramble out from underneath the cold battle. Every nerve in his body burned. He got to his feet, shaking, as the snarling and grunting of the warriors raged around him, and as he looked to the right and the left, he saw his army fighting on grimly, their hearts hard against Sammael's dreams.

Their faces showed nothing: no fear, no joy, no pity. They reached out to the dreams with their blackened weapons, cleaving them in two, severing heads from bodies, arms from hands. Sammael's dreams were many, but Danny's army was terrible, and the dreams might keep coming, but they couldn't win against *The Book of Shadows*.

Danny was afraid of his own warriors. Ori shone golden among them. She had thrown her head back and was baying, her barks and howls as eerie as those of a mountain wolf, calling to the moon. She was not looking at Danny any more.

'Ori!' he called in desperation, and the dog looked across the melee. Her lips stretched over her teeth in a ghoulish smile, and she caught his eye briefly before ducking down behind a group of fighters, so that he couldn't see her any more.

So that was it. Even Ori had deserted him at the last. All the dreams would die, and he would be left with his barren desert, and no space in *The Book of Shadows* to let him fill it with life. And he would have to call that victory. At least Sammael would die, in the end.

But even that was starting to sound awful, now.

How did I end up killing dreams, thought Danny. I'm supposed to be the hero, here.

Then he saw Ori again, ducking and weaving through the crowd, heading away from him. As the ranks slashed and surged, a gap opened up, and Danny watched the dog dodging swords and spears, leaping over the corpses of fallen fighters. Where was she going? Surely not towards –

Towards Sammael.

Danny's heart plunged into bleak despair. Why had he told Ori to go away? He hadn't meant it. She was his friend: his best, most loyal friend. Sammael or no Sammael, Ori had never harmed him. She had risked her own life to save his, and he had rejected her because he hated even the whisper of Sammael's name. Because he had been blind, bloody-minded, stubborn –

Ori bounced around another knot of soldiers, and swerved off to the left. As Danny watched, she dropped down so that her golden belly was on the desert sand, and then began to crawl. More soldiers clashed together, closing the gap, and Danny lost sight of the dog in the warring madness.

Please let her be safe, he begged. If only there was even an inch of space in *The Book of Shadows* for him to write it – but the pages were covered completely in his mad, scrawling writing, and the book had nothing more to give him.

He ducked under a swirling sword, escaping it easily. The blows didn't seem to be aimed at him – it seemed even Sammael wanted him still alive to witness the end of his stupidity. He wanted them to hit him, wanted to feel that he was at least getting hurt in this terrible, grim battle, and he was about to run screaming into a wall of waving spears when he caught sight of Ori again.

This time she was running towards him. She had something in her mouth, something small, and as she bounded through the falling soldiers, her lips were stretched back in the same grin.

She scrambled to a halt at Danny's feet, and offered the object up to him. He took it. Yet another book – slim, black-bound.

'What is it?'

'Sammael's book of sand. I stole it from his pocket.'

'His what?'

'His book of sand,' she repeated. 'Where he writes his bargains. Every single bargain he has ever made. It is the last piece of his power. Without it, he is lost.'

'You stole it from him? Why?'

And Ori gazed up at Danny, her face steady. 'So that you may win, if you choose.'

Danny gazed around, watching the ruthless sword thrusts and arrow volleys of his own slaughtering side. This was it. First he had taken Sammael's coat, then his boots, and now his notebook. This was the last piece of Sammael's power. This was what he had wanted all along.

He could stop the fight. His army would stop killing the dreams. Sammael would survive, but without any power to control Chromos. It was a perfect ending.

He scribbled out the last few incoherent lines in *The Book of Shadows*, raised Sammael's little book to the skies and shouted. 'Sammael! Lost anything?'

One by one Sammael's shadows raised their heads and lost them to the swinging swords of Danny's army. A whole line of them fell into the sand, and his army stepped forward to attack the ranks behind.

'Stop!' Danny commanded them. 'Cease!'

At his word the army stopped, swords raised, javelins held on their shoulders.

Sammael slid around the shadow of a great oak tree, scarred from dozens of sword blows. He stood before Danny.

'Need this?' asked Danny, keeping the book well away from Sammael's reach.

Sammael looked at Ori. 'That wasn't part of the bargain, my friend,' he said softly. 'I sent you to help him be brave, not to defeat me.'

So Ori had been telling the truth. Danny wanted to apologise to her, but there would be time for that later. Instead, he opened the little black book. It was covered in writing so tiny that he had to squint to read it.

He cleared his throat from the dust of battle and read aloud.

'"*I, Olaf Thorn, give freely my sand to Sammael, in exchange for the ability to walk.*"'

He looked at the creature in front of him, pale and waiting. 'To walk? Who was Olaf Thorn? Was he paralysed?'

'He was a blade of grass,' said Sammael.

'Grass doesn't walk,' said Danny.

Sammael shrugged.

Danny read the next one. '"*I, Secundus, give freely my sand to Sammael, in exchange for my safe passage in the conquering of the Northern World.*" Who was Secundus?'

'A soldier,' said Sammael.

'When? What was the Northern World?'

Again, Sammael shrugged. 'It's none of your business. Those are pacts creatures made with their lives. They aren't silly stories for you to crow at. You should return that to me.'

'Not likely,' Danny snorted. 'Without this, you're finished. No sand, no nothing. If I tore this book up . . .' He held it out, a hand on each side, and went as if to rip it down the spine.

Sammael gasped. It was a sound of pain and sorrow and the deepest regret.

Danny grinned and stopped his hands. 'That's it,' he said. 'I've got you. Shall I do it?'

Sammael stood, white faced, and then some of the old hardness came into his black eyes, and he was strong again, resilient. 'All things have their time,' he said. 'If mine is over, so be it.'

Danny's triumph faded. He wanted Sammael to beg, to plead, to apologise for everything he'd done. He wanted Sammael to tell him that he, Danny, was right, and his vision for the world was a good one.

But Sammael would never say that, of course.

'It is,' said Danny. 'It is over. You're finished. I'll never dream about you again, and nor will anybody else. And if someone wants to sell their soul, they'll have to find another way to do it. I'm going to rip this book into confetti.'

'Go on, then,' said Sammael. 'Have the courage of your convictions. Tear it up.'

Danny tightened his fingers around the little book. It felt like something he remembered – snakeskin? Not snakeskin, but some kind of skin, definitely. Rabbit skin? No, it wasn't that soft. Human skin? For a moment, he shuddered.

But it wasn't that. It was a little softer still. Perhaps the delicate furred skin on Shimny's nose. It reminded him of Ori's ears. Of his parents, and Tom. Of all the things that made his heart sing.

He cleared his throat again and spat on the ground, hoping it would seem like he was just spitting out more battle dust.

'What's it made of?' he asked, trying to stop his cheeks flaming up.

'I told you,' said Sammael. 'It's made of creatures who wanted to change the world. They wanted to know more, to see further. They entrusted themselves to me and I gave them what they wanted. In the end, each and every one of them made the whole miserable world of Xur into a better place, even if just for a single, blazing second. Why do you think their dreams fought with so much heart against you? You're trying to destroy all the hope they ever believed in.'

'Shut up!' Danny felt his voice wavering with uncertainty. Sammael was trying to confuse him again. He needed to keep his head clear, follow his original plans. He had Sammael's book. All he had to do was destroy it . . .

Deliberately looking away from Sammael, he tried not to think about any of the things that had just been said. He twisted the little book between his hands and tugged at one half, pushing at the other.

'Danny!'

Of all the voices in the world, it was the only one that could have stopped him. In front of her – if she saw what he was doing, if she realised he was tearing up Sammael's last power . . .

He'd see her face, and he'd never be able to live with himself.

'Danny!'

What was she even doing here? She should still be on earth, waiting to be summoned to the new world along with everybody else.

He turned around.

She was sitting astride a red and gold horse, a horse that shone brighter than any polished sword. The hare, Barshin, was tucked into her chest. Both were covered in a flowing cloak that seemed to hold all the colours Danny had ever seen in his life – apart, he thought, from a few greens found around the edge of the school playing field – and they carried something with them, draped over the horse's withers. It was long and pale, and it appeared to weigh very little, for Cath had her hand on it and was holding it firmly down.

She was thin and dirty, and dark shadows sat in the hollows of her grey cheeks. Wherever she had travelled, it had clearly cost her.

And then she smiled, and her face reflected the yellow of the sunshine and the blue of the sky.

'We've got him,' she said. 'We've found him. You can have him back.'

Danny's eyes went to the pale lump dangling down the horse's shoulder. And although he knew the answer, he swallowed hard and croaked, through the lump in his throat, 'Who?'

'Tom,' said Cath. 'We've brought him back for you.'

Chapter 21

Tom

Danny lifted the pale body down from the horse's back. It weighed nothing at all, and felt as papery as the dream version of Kalia that he'd once brought out of Chromos to fool Sammael with.

He laid it on the desert sand and forced himself to look at it.

It was Tom. Not the shining, lively cousin he had once known, the staunch friend who had taken him on so many adventures, who had always been ready with a sandwich and a slice of pie, dragging him out into the midnight woods. Not the tall, clever companion who knew every path and tree for miles around, who could knock a fence post in with three blows of a sledgehammer or wrestle a fractious cow to the ground.

It was something left of Tom's body. A fragile structure held together by light and dreams. Tom's soul.

'Where did you find him?' he managed to say, as Cath slid down from the red and gold horse, clutching the coloured cloak around her.

'The aether,' Cath said. And that was all.

'How?' Danny asked her, but she had lost her smile, and shrugged.

'You know the earth's burning up?' she said.

'It's OK,' he said. 'I've got this now. I'll scribble out what I wrote in *The Book of Shadows* and we can go back to earth. Nothing bad will happen there any more.'

He held up Sammael's book for them all to see. Even though Barshin must have seen it before, Cath, Shimny and the hare all shrank back from it. Only Ori remained close to Danny, solid and trusting at his side.

None of them spoke.

'It's Sammael's,' said Danny, into the empty air. 'He can't get any more sand without it.'

Barshin struggled out of Cath's arms and landed at Danny's feet. Grey and dusty, he blended into the desert as if he'd been sculpted from it.

'We braved great fears to bring you Tom,' said the hare, looking up at Danny. 'You must honour us by facing him, and deciding what to do. Where do you think he should go?'

Danny couldn't answer for a moment. He looked at Sammael's book again. So many pages. That tiny, spidery writing, covering the thin paper. Who would he find in there, if he read the whole thing? Olaf Thorn. Secundus. An old man called Abel Korsakov. Barshin. Ori.

He turned to the last pages of writing. It must be there –
And then he found it.

Tom's bargain.

'*I, Tom Fletcher, give freely my sand . . .*'

His eyes stung with a sharp pain. If only be had been there to stop Tom from signing it. If only he had managed to get in the way somehow. If only he had been able to bring Tom back, the real Tom, gentle and bright and alive.

But Tom's life had been lived and it had ended, and that was the hard, solid truth.

'I don't know,' he said, eventually. His voice wouldn't rise above a whisper. 'I don't know where he should go. What do you think?'

He turned his eyes on the hare. Without Barshin, Tom would still be alive, but Danny didn't even blame Barshin, now. He was too tired and confused to blame anybody. Tom was dead, and that was it.

'You have two choices,' said Barshin. 'Either leave his sand to Sammael, as he wished, or make your own bargain with Sammael, and ask for Tom's soul back. Then return it to Death, and she will put it into the earth, as you wish.'

'Sammael's powerless now!' said Danny. 'And Tom didn't want to be with him, anyway. It was a trick. Tom didn't know anything about Chromos, or the colours, or any of that. He just wanted to be able to talk to birds and animals.'

'You must accept,' said Barshin gravely, 'that Tom made his bargain freely, according to the desire in his heart. He may not even have been able to spell out what it was. But it was inside him, and it drove him. May I tell you, briefly, what happened to me?'

Danny shrugged. 'I know you lost your girlfriend, then you made a bargain with Sammael – probably that one day you'd see her again, I guess. Isn't that it?'

'My love, Marija, was a champion boxer,' said Barshin. 'A true champion, whose lightness of paw pulled her high above ordinary hares, and secured her a place among the very stars. She was as nimble as a spider casting out its first thread, swinging weightless into the air in search of a distant anchor. I loved her, and she loved me. But when I met her, her soul was not her own. She had given it already to Sammael, in return for her boxing skills.'

'So she wasn't that great, really, was she?' said Danny. 'She just bought her skill.'

'A great fighter requires an even greater opponent,' said Barshin, his voice so tight that it threatened to snap in two. 'The better one is, the more others must progress. In that way, skills advance, and everyone benefits. But while some work on their skill, others prefer to profit by deceit. Marija took on an opponent who had laid a trap in the ground. She fell into it, and he . . . he killed her. For months, I was plagued by dreams about her: that she was still alive, that she came back to me. But gradually another figure began to creep into those dreams . . .'

'Sammael,' said Danny. 'Yeah, he gets about in dreams, doesn't he?'

'Sammael,' agreed Barshin. 'He gave me the chance to look into the darkest corners of my mind. I began to recall stories Marija had whispered in my ear as I slept. I remembered the way she twitched her ears sometimes, listening to silence. And I began to understand that Marija had not returned to the earth, but left her spirit in the hands of another. And I could get no peace.

'So I sought out Sammael for myself, and I asked him for Marija's soul back. I wanted to return her to the earth. I wanted to lie down and press myself to the soil and feel close to her, and know that the worms were singing her songs. I wanted to know where she was.

'As you know, I made a bargain with him. I freely gave up my own sand to him and I agreed to try and trap you, in exchange for the promise that once the business was concluded, Marija's sand would be returned to the earth. So now we come to the point where I should be asking one final favour of you.'

Danny stared at the hare. 'I don't owe you anything,' he said. 'Nothing at all.'

'Indeed you don't,' said Barshin. 'But you now hold the soul of my beloved Marija in your hand. Sammael needs his book in order to release her.'

'So? That's not my problem. You should have got her ages ago.'

'Nevertheless. While you have that book, Marija is in limbo, and Tom is in limbo. Only Sammael can release their sand from the bargains they made with him.'

Danny looked around at the armies, the sky, the sand, his tiny bunch of friends, and Tom on the ground.

The fragile case of Tom, waiting to become something new.

Tom hadn't tried to improve the world. He had only loved it. He would have wanted Danny to do what was best for it, to rid it of Sammael, even if it meant that he, Tom, had to stay in limbo forever . . .

Wouldn't he?

And Danny realised that he didn't know. He had never asked Tom what he wanted, and he couldn't now. He had to decide for them both.

He looked up at the sky. There were no birds in it, apart from the weary, exhausted birds of his army and Sammael's dreams, and both those sets of birds were sitting sullenly on any perches they could find – heads, spears, shield rims.

Danny remembered the skylarks on the farm, soaring above the fields, their endlessly jumbled songs patterning the sky. He recalled the crows and jays, the blackbirds, the gulls, the pigeons. Tom had loved all the birds. Perhaps he would like to stay with them?

But he had loved the cows too. And the badgers. Those slow, lumbering creatures of the soil, who rooted around for insects, shuffling through the darkness. Cows were only a brief jump into the air between two earthbound ends. Badgers were the same – barely even a jump – their noses and tails sunk into the soil.

'The earth,' he said. 'Tom belongs to the earth. He always did.'

Barshin said, very gently, 'But only Sammael can release him from that book. So what are you going to do?'

Danny looked down at the book. For a second he wavered. He couldn't give the book back to Sammael, surely? It would restore some of his power. And then Sammael might just take Tom's soul and burn open Chromos with it, and refuse to honour any pledge Danny had managed to get out of him.

He looked up at Sammael. There was no trace of emotion on the creature's face. If anything, there was a concentrated blandness.

I'm done for, thought Danny. I don't know how this power works, or what to use it for. I blundered into this entirely by mistake, a long time ago. And I never really wanted to rule the entire universe. I just want to do what's best for Tom.

Sammael smiled, very thinly indeed.

'In that case,' he said. 'I'd like my book back, please. And while you're about it, I'll have your soul, too.'

Chapter 22

The Bargain

'No!' Danny gripped the book. That couldn't be right. There must be some way he could give the book back, or learn how to use it, without having to give himself to Sammael. That was the thing he'd sworn he'd never do.

'That's the bargain,' said Sammael. 'You give me back my book, and you give your sand to me. Otherwise everything stays as it is. Your cousin stays as he is, and you live with it. Your choice.'

That would be OK, wouldn't it? Danny looked at the carapace of Tom, lying on the sand. It would be OK to just leave him there and get on with building the new world, building a new Tom . . .

And the claws of all that he had learnt over the past weeks and months rose up from the sand and plucked at his shoulders, dragging them down. He couldn't build a new Tom, and he couldn't forget the old one.

He choked on the dryness in his throat and had to draw

hard at the air to breathe. It reminded him of being in the aether. 'How do I know you won't take his sand and use it to break open Chromos again?'

'I never break promises,' said Sammael. 'Right or wrong, I never break them. Once they're written down, I leave the rest to the legends and the stars.'

Legends. Danny looked at the book in his hand, and drew out his own again from his pocket. Two legendary books, and he held them both.

There had been too many books and stories in this journey. He couldn't know if any of them had even a grain of truth in them any more. He had come to the end of the final page.

His leg shuffled sideways against Ori's bulk, and he looked around for Cath, but she had sunk to her knees in the sand and was clutching Barshin. They were as grey as dusk.

His friends.

'Can you save them?' he asked Sammael.

Sammael shook his black-curled head. 'You closed me off from Chromos,' he said. 'I can't do anything for them now, unless I find a way to get back in there.'

Tom. Cath. Barshin.

What about his parents? If he agreed to give himself up to Sammael, they would lose another child.

So many lives, all in Danny's hands.

He closed his eyes and held out Sammael's little book. 'I'll do it,' he said. The words felt like stones, dropping down his throat. 'You can have my sand, if you give me

Tom's. And I want enough time to give Tom to Death so she can put him into the earth, and I want to save Cath and Barshin. That's all. After that, you can kill me and use my sand for whatever you like. I won't know. I won't care. As long as you make sure my parents don't know anything about it.'

'What a hero,' said Sammael. He took the offered book. As it left Danny's hand, Danny felt a hundred times lighter. There was nothing to fight for any more. He knew what was going to happen, and that was it. The hand went instinctively to Ori's golden head, and her fur under his palm was soft.

Sammael wrote something in the book and showed it to Danny. It read:

'*I, Danny O'Neill, do freely give my sand to Sammael, in exchange for the sand of Tom Fletcher, which I shall give to Death. Also in return I shall receive sufficient time to enable me to restore Cath Carrera and Barshin the hare to a good and flourishing state of health. My endeavours on earth shall be confined to these two acts. Signed:*'

Danny shrugged and signed it.

Sammael gave a brief nod. 'I'd better go and put the fires out on Earth,' he said. 'I'll come and find you when you're finished. Don't bother trying to hide.'

Danny hadn't even considered it. He had already assumed there wouldn't be any point. Sammael owned him now. Of course he would be able to find Danny, wherever he was.

And then Sammael turned his back on Danny and faced his army of dreams.

'Retreat,' he commanded them. 'This world is finished. Return to Earth and quench the sun's flames. Earth needs its dreams.'

And the shadow army and its commander melted away, leaving only the five creatures on Danny's half-created world of sand.

It was only then that Danny realised the red and gold horse was his old friend Shimny. He put his head in his hands and said, through his scratched palms, 'What have I done to everyone?'

'They're all like us,' said Cath.

'All who?' Danny raised his eyes, squinting against the unfiltered sun.

'All the people on Earth, who got caught under the shadows. They're all still grey. All the places, too. Even after Sammael puts the fires out, they'll still be grey. The colour's not coming back.'

'Of course it'll come back,' said Danny. 'Sammael will see to that. Let's go and find Death, so I can give Tom to her. And you just need more gorse. I'll find gorse for you, so you're better again.'

Cath shook her head. 'The gorse wears off. It reaches my skin, but not my heart. And it doesn't work for Barshin.'

'Good,' said Danny. 'Then I can live forever, pretending I'm trying to find a cure for him, can't I?'

'That's not keeping your side of the bargain, though,' said Cath. 'So Sammael won't have to keep his, will he?'

'Well, what'll cure you, then?' said Danny, although he had a feeling he might know the answer.

'We've got to put Chromos back on Earth,' said Cath.

'Oh, yeah? And how do we do that? Use Tom's sand to burn it open ourselves?'

Cath shook her head. 'Sammael's the only one who knows how to put Chromos onto sand so it can spread properly.'

'But Sammael can't do that any more,' said Danny, slowly. 'We saw to that – you and me. None of us can go back there, either.'

'We can,' said Cath. She touched the cloak around her shoulders. In comparison to her greyness, it was brighter than a rainbow. 'We came here through Chromos. Barshin, Shimny and me. My cloak protected us.'

'Where did you get it?'

'I made it.'

'So you reckon we should call Sammael back and give him that cloak, so he can get up to Chromos again?' Danny couldn't believe she was even hinting at it. Had all this fighting really been for nothing?

But that wasn't what Cath was saying. What she was saying was even worse.

'We've got to go there ourselves. We need to get his boots back and give them to him. He's the world's imagination, Danny. The world needs him. Don't you get it yet?'

And Danny's heart sank to the russet sands at his feet. He knew that she was right. Sammael had been the most frightening thing in his life for too long now. But without fear, he would still have been in his house, waiting for his parents to come home. He would never have met Cath, or

Isbjin al-Orr, or had any of the adventures that had come his way. He would never even have learnt Shimny's name.

Sammael's heart favoured neither pain nor happiness: both were equal to him. He spread fear and chaos, but he also spread the infinite colours of novelty and hope. They were all scary, when you faced them at first and saw how powerless you were to control them. But sometimes fear wasn't altogether the enemy.

Cath was right. The only solution was to restore Sammael's chaos to the world. Cath and Barshin would regain their colour and their lives. Tom would properly die. And Danny would disappear.

For a moment Danny felt an agony so terrible it seemed to burst his stomach. But when he looked down, nothing had changed. His stomach was intact and full, and he was fine. The pain came from nothing more than regret, and there was no way around that now. He had signed Sammael's book.

I wonder if . . . he caught himself thinking, and then he closed the thought firmly down.

'Chromos, then,' he said. 'For the last time.'

There was no trouble in Chromos. There were no shadows. They travelled up smoothly on Shimny's crowded back, Danny, Cath, dog, hare and a new addition: the paper-light corpse of Tom. Wisps of darkness floated around the corpse, as if Chromos had something a little nasty to say about the sand body it couldn't yet touch, but none of the darkness came near Danny. The world was great and green, and the sky was wide. It was exactly as Danny had seen it the time he'd fled home on Zadoc, after leaving Cath behind on the beach.

Then, he'd been full of hope for the future. And even though his head knew now that all the hope was gone, his heart felt the tug of it, and opened up, wide and shining. What more was there to want? This – this was freedom, pure and simple.

Chromos was being kind to him. And one day soon, he would die, and have to leave it all.

At this thought, he expected the great plain to darken and boil. But it stayed calm, emerald and glorious and wild, and he realised that he didn't fear dying any more. One day, Chromos promised him, one day soon you'll join me. And his heart was full of joy at the promise.

Not so his head. His head raged on. It was impossible – to die and leave everything so unresolved. His parents would never know what had happened to him. He hoped he'd been nice enough to them. And Cath wouldn't forget him. She'd managed to remember Tom. Danny was sure she would do the same for him.

He felt an urge to be nice to her, so that he could be sure of leaving at least one good account of himself on Earth.

'Where do you think we'll find the boots?' he asked her. 'Shall we imagine up the sun chariot again?'

They had destroyed the boots by throwing them off the back of Apollo's chariot into the burning sun. Perhaps Cath had other ideas, though. Danny braced himself for her scorn.

But Cath was gentle, her tone soft. 'Let's not go back to old stories,' she said. 'Let's at least make something new this time.'

Danny was wary of that. Hadn't he already tried, with The Book of Shadows? Fat lot of good that had done.

Still, there was no point in being faint-hearted. Not any more.

'Sure,' he said. 'Let's make our own boots. Let's imagine up Xur, and kill him ourselves, and make them out of his hide.'

'Maybe not even Xur,' said Cath.

'But he's the one whose skin has the special power, isn't he?'

Cath nodded. 'So do other things, now, though. My cloak. Zadoc.'

'Zadoc! What if we made them out of Zadoc?' said Danny, feeling the strong hoofbeats of the ghost horse come drifting in a memory across the plain, way out to his right. 'Except Zadoc's gone.'

But nothing was really gone in Chromos. Everything could be brought back, in some kind of a way. So he opened his mouth and added, 'Though maybe we could bring him back?'

And they were on a parched, rocky landscape, with thorny acacia trees and tough scrubby bushes, following a thin trickle of water that ran between boulders, down towards a cavern. In front of the cavern, Zadoc grazed, with a handful of cream-coloured mares at his side. As they approached, Shimny stepped her way neatly around the rocks and scrub, her golden hooves crunching against dry twigs.

Zadoc threw up his head and whinnied to her, and Shimny answered back. The horses stared at each other, testing the air for scent, but Shimny kept walking as she sniffed, her ribs drawing sharply in and out.

It was that easy, then. Danny just had to think of Zadoc and another task was complete, and he was another step closer to his own death. Too easy. But he had given up hoping for any delays. Obstacles only stood in the way when you didn't want them there. Everything including Chromos, it seemed, wanted to smooth his path into Sammael's hands.

They were almost close enough to touch Zadoc when Danny noticed the figure in the mouth of the cavern, half hidden in its shadow.

An old man. Older than any person Danny had ever seen, with a yellowish, wispy beard and a maze of discontented wrinkles spread over his face. His eyes were hard and blue.

And Danny knew him.

He had died a year and a half ago, in front of Danny's own face. More than died. He had taken hold of the taro, and been eaten up by white fire.

Abel Korsakof.

For a long time, Danny had seen his face in nightmares. But Abel Korsakof had belonged to Sammael. He should have been in Sammael's shadow army. What was he doing here?

Shimny halted, and Danny looked down at the old man.

'Why are you here?' he asked. 'I didn't imagine you up. I wasn't even thinking about you.'

'I chose to die,' said Abel Korsakof. 'I took hold of the power of the storm. I knew at the end that I belonged not to Sammael, but to the storm. And I chose the storm. You knew this. You saw it happen.'

And then Abel Korsakof vanished, as quickly as he had appeared.

To Danny, the words felt like the last piece in a huge puzzle. But the puzzle itself was so vast that he couldn't stand back far enough to see the whole of it. He needed to raise himself high above the world and look at it from a great distance; only then would he be able to understand what all these things meant.

I'll get the chance soon enough, he thought. Soon, it will all be over for me. There'll be nothing more to add.

He felt Cath's hand tugging at his waist.

'What shall we do?' she asked him. 'I don't want to kill Zadoc.'

Danny looked at the great brown-grey horse. He didn't want to kill Zadoc either. He didn't really want anything to ever have to die again, least of all himself.

'Let's talk to him,' he said. 'He was our friend. We should tell him what we want.'

Zadoc, unbidden, left his mares and came stepping towards them, covering the small distance in only a couple of his giant strides.

'We thought you'd dissolved,' said Danny. 'You were a ghost last time I saw you.'

'I am a ghost,' replied the great horse. 'Chromos has no guardian any more. I am here only because you see me here.'

A horrible thought occurred to Danny. 'If we take you out of Chromos, will you just disappear, like Kalia?' he asked.

But at that, the horse dipped his head. 'You wish to restore Sammael's boots to him. You destroyed them in Chromos, so you can remake them in here. If you take me out, I shall surely disappear. But if you can take the boots out – they will last beyond eternity. They will be made of your desire and your hope.'

'Won't they be the same boots as before?'

'No. Nothing can be the same forever. Nothing can be the same for even a very short time. Everything changes, always.'

'So we should make the new boots out of you?'

Zadoc moved his great head close to Danny's face. For the first time, Danny became aware of the heavy scent of horse: sweat and herbs and hair.

'Do you think you can?'

Danny nodded, without needing to hesitate.

'Why are you so sure?' asked the horse.

And the words came, unthought, from Danny's heart. 'Because it's not Chromos that needs you as a Guardian: it's our world. Every single creature on earth should have a Zadoc, so they can sit on his back and see the world the way they dream it could be. Sammael needs to keep feeding the colours down, so that the stars keep shining and the storms keep raging, and we all keep knowing that things can change, if only we change what's in our heads. Sammael will terrify us, and he'll hurt us, and he won't care. But we need to keep having new ideas, and new dreams. I can make Sammael's boots again, because I know that the world needs him.'

He broke off, and knew that he had spoken from his heart, not his head: he was still very afraid of Sammael, and he still thought that Sammael lacked something very important, which was called kindness. But his heart stayed steady and strong. He couldn't control the world any more. He could only love it, and want the best for it.

And Zadoc understood. 'It won't be messy,' he said. 'You'll know what to do.'

Danny knew. He watched it happen: the sky darkened, and Zadoc snorted in alarm, calling his mares to him with a high-pitched whinny. Together, the small band of horses cantered across the face of the cavern and up a rocky path along the cliff face, rising to the cliff top above Danny's head. But when they reached the cliff top, instead of staying together, the mares raced away and Zadoc stopped, silhouetted against the dark orange sky.

The horse waited patiently as the clouds swam together above him. Thunder grumbled and belched, and small rocks fell from the cliff face, bouncing down to lie at Shimny's feet. Danny was no longer afraid of storms: he sat upright like Cath behind him, one arm wrapped around Ori, the other on the cloak draped over their little band. Perhaps it was only the shelter of the cloak that had made him unafraid?

No. He would never be afraid of storms again. This one was coming from inside him. He, too, was a child of the storms.

Then the lightning came. His own lightning. He sent it down from the sky – there! There! He sent it cracking down into the rocks around Zadoc, and the horse did not flinch but stood patiently, waiting to be struck.

Danny threw the biggest bolt of lightning down onto Zadoc's knobbly grey-brown head, and Zadoc fell to the ground with relief.

Chapter 23

The Boots

They waited for the storm to roll away, then went up to find Zadoc, Shimny picking her way carefully up the narrow cliff path. The lightning had done its work: Zadoc was nothing more than a shrivelled, dried-up hide, stained the jet black of burnt embers.

Danny reached down to pick up the hide. He needed no warnings about staining himself with the things he touched in Chromos. Zadoc was already a part of him.

He knew what to do with the hide. Cath had a knife, but it was scarcely needed: the pieces fell away from each other, as though the whole hide was just a template, ready-scored, for a pair of knee-high boots.

They used the sail needle from the boatshed. They made threads again, with Cath's hair. They put together thick pads of leather for the soles, and the needle went through as though holes had already been punched for it.

Danny and Cath made a boot each.

'I'll do the left one,' said Cath, grinning. Danny let her do it. It felt good, working together for the same thing, knowing that there wasn't any need to disagree or quarrel. Or even to speak much, except to pass between them the knife, needle and thread.

At last the boots were made. They looked at each other, sitting on the red and gold of Shimny's back.

For a brief second, they looked at the boots they each held, then back at each other.

'Nice job,' said Cath. 'Well done.'

Danny nodded briefly, turning over the boot he held. It was strange to think of it existing long after he had gone. Probably long after even the soil and the worms had forgotten him, this boot would still be travelling the universe.

He felt another strong urge to stay alive, but he squashed it far down inside him. He knew the truth, now – the boot would be all that was left of him, and it would belong to Sammael.

Danny made himself smile at Cath. At least she'll be a bit happy, he thought. That's something.

'Let's take Tom home, then,' he said. 'And find Death.'

As they touched down back at Sopper's Edge, Danny slipped off Shimny, pulled down Ori and Tom's corpse, and stood looking up at Cath.

'Will you go and give Sammael the boots?' he asked. 'I don't want to see his face when he knows I made one. I don't want to see him looking smug.'

'He'll know already,' said Cath. 'Besides, I don't reckon he'll be smug. He does love the world in his own way, you know.'

Danny didn't agree, but he didn't want to argue. He wanted to say goodbye to Tom.

'Even so,' he said. 'I've got stuff to do.'

Cath nodded, and didn't ask further. That was definitely one of the best things about Cath. She knew a lot.

'Where do you want to meet up?' she said, suddenly.

It was an unexpected question. Danny hadn't been thinking any further than Tom, and what he was about to do. But he realised all at once that this was the end of the journey for him and Cath. They had no need of each other any more. Once Sammael had his boots back, Cath would quickly regain her colour along with Barshin and the rest of the world. And Danny would have all he had asked for.

He would never again sit in a boring Geography lesson, stare out of the window and catch himself thinking of the wild journey he had been on, and the wild girl he had met. He would never dream of what might have happened to her, or wonder if he would ever see her again. All those moments when her scorn had helped him to find courage were gone, forever.

This was it.

They were saying goodbye.

As he looked into her steady black eyes, he could do nothing more than shrug, and wish he'd had a little bit more time to make friends with her. They'd never agreed on much.

But at least they'd been true to themselves. We had to fight with each other, thought Danny. Cath is brave and determined, and I am weak and scared. Why should she ever have liked me? Why did she even bother to help me?

And he knew that he could never figure out the answers to those questions now. He had run out of time.

Sun broke through the clouds. Danny forced himself to smile. He made his face as broad, as confident as possible. It felt very unnatural.

'Oh, I don't know where we'll meet next,' he said. 'I'm sure we'll run into each other again. We always do, don't we?'

Cath opened her mouth to reply, thought better of it, and shrugged.

'OK then. See you around.'

Danny couldn't say any more. He stooped, picked up Tom's fragile corpse, and turned away.

He headed straight up to the top of the hill towards the wood, with Ori bounding beside him. He didn't want to run the risk of running into Aunt Kathleen – he wasn't ready to find out what had happened to her, yet.

And he didn't want to watch Shimny, Barshin and Cath go.

At the far edge of Hangman's Wood, Danny found a spot where he could see over the valley beyond, and sat on a fallen tree trunk at the edge of the wood. Ori sat quietly on the ground beside him, close enough for him to rest a hand on her golden coat.

The afternoon was drawing on into evening. Shadows stretched long across the land below, clawing away the daylight. Danny watched them growing, inching over the fields and houses. What a shame he'd never sat here and watched them before.

There's so much of the world I'll never know, thought Danny. I wish –

But he was sitting and waiting for Death to take his cousin, and another kind of death to take him, and wishes were pointless now.

Death came at sunset, just as the shadows had grown wide into a blanket of dusk. Her eyes were red and her grey hair was tangled about her face, and she trod as wearily as a soldier trying to find the way home after battle.

Ori hid her face in Danny's trousers, but Danny had no need to turn away. He watched Death's eyes and her wrinkled old skin, and he found himself smiling at the patient sigh she gave as she came to stand in front of him.

'You,' she said.

Danny nodded. He didn't fear her any more. She was just a tired old woman. Besides which, she had come to free Tom.

Death looked down at Tom's body, and then at Danny.

'Should I ask what you gave up to get him?'

Danny shook his head.

'You humans,' she said. 'Full of strange ideas about nobility. You look after others better than you look after yourselves. That's your idea of a good human, isn't it?'

Danny didn't want to talk to her about that.

'What'll you do with him?' he asked.

'Return him to the soil, of course. That's what I do.'

234

'And people will remember him?'

'Of course.' Death nodded. 'They'll assume he died in some kind of accident, I'd think. Even if they're not entirely sure, they'll soon think of a story and convince themselves it's true.'

'And he'll be at peace?'

Death laughed. 'He won't be anything. There won't be a Tom any more. It's you who needs peace, isn't it? If it helps you to find it, then I'll tell you that he will. He'll be a part of all life. That's the kind of peace he'll have.'

Danny thought of the farm, and the woods and fields and birds and badgers, all together with Tom.

'He'd like that,' he said.

'You'd like that,' said Death. 'Why did you give yourself up to Sammael? Do you understand what he's getting from you?'

'Yeah.' Danny nodded. 'But I didn't have a choice, in the end.'

'Of course you did,' said Death.

Danny shrugged. 'I could have left Tom behind. I could have left bits of the world grey, and pretended not to see them. But I'd never have stopped thinking about it.'

'Poor boy,' said Death. 'There's a lot on your shoulders.'

Danny didn't feel sorry for himself. It wasn't that hard to face things, when they were so inevitable.

'Why do people do it?' he asked, looking up into Death's red eyes. 'Why do they give themselves to him freely, when they don't have to? I still don't understand that.'

'Ach, I don't know,' said Death. 'To me, it is only right and proper that things come from the earth and return to the earth. But there is a power in imagination that lifts creatures out of the earth, higher and higher, until their toes are dangling in the stars. They live in the coloured sky, and they throw handfuls of it down to remind the rest of earth's creatures to raise their eyes once in a while. They give up their own lives in the belief that they can improve the world – not by violence or death, or hurt, but by dreaming wonderful dreams, and thinking up glorious ideas, and passing them down to others. Sammael would tell you that life begins not on earth, but in dreams. I would not agree with him. But I honour him for saying it.'

'What about Abel Korsakof?' asked Danny, remembering the old man's strange words in Chromos. 'Who got him, in the end? It was Sammael, wasn't it?'

Death looked confused for a moment, as if struggling to remember, and then her soft old face went curiously beautiful.

'Ah no,' she said. 'Abel Korsakof has long returned to his Polish soil, and if he could know anything, he would know what peace was now.'

Danny frowned as the last fragment of sun slipped below the horizon. 'But he sold his soul to Sammael, didn't he? How did he get out of it?'

'That, I don't know,' said Death. 'I only know that I was summoned to him, and when I found him, he was mine. The reasons were unfathomable.'

Danny's heart, which had given a little leap, sank again. 'Well,' he said. 'Here is Tom. I guess you'd better take him.'

Death stooped and gathered up Tom in her arms. He did not look weightless any more; he hung in her embrace as if he were a young man again, asleep, his limbs dangling with their full, muscled heaviness.

Danny tried to say goodbye, but his voice didn't work.

And Death turned away to walk off down the valley side. His eyes wouldn't follow her for long: soon she became impossible to see through the darkness, and he knew that he had had his last sight of both of them. He would never see Tom again. Nor would he ever rest his eyes on the friendly old face of Death. Fate had something altogether different in store for him.

He touched the solid earth beneath his feet and wanted to throw himself down onto it. It seemed so unfair that Barshin the hare claimed the earth as his own element. It was Danny who wanted to cling to it, Danny who felt every grain inside him calling out to the soil, longing to be a part of it again.

But I am water, he told himself. Water evaporates. It has to let go, and fly free.

Angrily, he pulled the useless *Book of Shadows* from his pocket and went to tear it up, to finish his connection with the whole, hated business, so that he could lie on the earth and close his eyes and wait for what was coming to him.

A drop of rain fell onto his face, out of the darkness.

Come on, he said to it. Soak me. Bring your friend the wind to knock me from side to side. Bring white forks of lightning to strike me from the skies. Make me feel alive one last time.

'Are you sure?' asked the splattered raindrop, as it trickled down his cheek.

Yes, I'm sure, he said, clutching *The Book of Shadows*. He could write no new worlds in it now, but it was still a taro, and he could still use it to speak with. Even if it was only minutes till he saw Sammael again, he had his voice for a little while longer.

He raised his mind to the darkened sky. And then he heard it, in the distance.

Thunder.

His heart leapt. His whole body threw all the hope and laughter it still held out towards the storm and yelled to it – Come on! Come and find me! I'm here, at Hangman's Wood!

And the storm came.

The rain fell harder, driving into his face with icy spears. The wind slammed against him, dragging at his clothes, whipping his frozen skin. Hail blinded him, thunder crashed against the trees of Hangman's Wood, roaring out in anger as the trees wailed in grief.

Danny watched the hail and the rain and the black branches of the trees swinging wildly in the black night; every flash of white lightning stung the world into a thousand swirling particles of ice and water and steam, and the fingers of the trees were the fingers of all that he was leaving behind: the life of the world, the rage of it, the frenzied, fantastic dance of it. And he knew the final thing about being alive: it was a storm – a terrifying, glorious storm – and you could never stay still because the winds would push you and the rain would soak you and there would always be hail to hide from and lightning to marvel at. And you could never be sure when you'd have to take shelter as it all became too fierce, or when you'd manage to stand fast against it, holding out against the powers that raged around you, trying to throw you in every direction.

Humans could never hold the lightning. They could only hold the trees and the earth and each other.

'Ori!' he shouted. 'Go! Into the woods! Go away!'

The dog cringed against his leg. 'I won't leave you,' she whimpered.

He shook her off. She had to leave him. He had to be alone.

'Go!' he shouted. 'I want you to go!'

'I'll wait for you,' she said. 'On the other side of the wood. I'll wait for you till you come.'

'I won't come!' shouted Danny. 'Don't wait for me. Go back to your old owner! Live a long and happy life! Go, and goodbye!'

Ori slunk away into the trees; he didn't see where she'd gone, and knew only that she had left him, and that he had said his last goodbye. Perhaps Sammael was coming for him in this storm? Perhaps the end wasn't far off.

But Danny couldn't feel Sammael's presence in the air. He was alone in the storm: himself and his book and some words he had to remember, some words he'd heard only recently –

'*I knew at the end, that I belonged . . . to the storm. And I chose the storm . . .*"

Abel Korsakof. He took hold of the lightning, and he let it kill him. And he belonged not to Sammael, but to the storm . . .

Danny turned his face to the sky and held the book up to it, and opened his heart to everything in it: the rain, the hail, the wind, the lightning . . .

And he knew.

Strike me, he said. Strike me down. I understand about Sammael. I understand about the earth. I choose that which I don't understand. I choose the storm.

The lightning struck around him, hissing and shrieking at the flailing trees. And he remembered that the taro protected him.

So he dropped *The Book of Shadows*.

The lightning struck him.

Danny O'Neill's body flew backwards against an ancient beech tree.

And his soul walked into the storm.

Chapter 24

The Guardians of Chromos

'Will he come?' Cath squatted in the lee of the dunes, looking out across the ink-dark sea.

'He'll come.'

Barshin kept close beside her, and she felt his wind-blown fur warm against the palm of her hand. His body was steady.

The gold of Shimny's coat cast some light around the beach, but not enough to see the house inland. Cath didn't want to see it anyway. She didn't belong here any more. But it had seemed like the best place to find Sammael again, so they had come back.

This beach was the closest she had ever had to a home. You need to look at something that feels like a broader part of yourself, Barshin had said. Open up your heart, and he'll hear you calling him.

And so they waited, as the light left the sky and the darkness rolled overhead, and it felt to Cath, too, like the end of a long journey. What lay beyond giving the boots to Sammael? She had no idea. Colour would come back to the grey parts of the earth, but a mere dusting of Chromos had never been enough for her. She wanted to feel herself soaked in it.

'There he is,' said Barshin.

He came with his own light around him, day still clinging to his shoulders, fending off the darkness and the shadows. He looked thin and old and tired, and his bare feet sank into the sand. His head was down and his face was hard to see, until he stood before Cath and turned his full gaze upon her. Then she saw that, however dusty and moth-eaten the rest of him might look, his black eyes were still bright. It was a soft, sparking brightness, and it refused utterly the suggestion that Sammael's hope would ever die.

'What now?' he asked.

Cath got to her feet and held out the boots.

'We made them,' she said. 'Both of us. One each.'

Sammael didn't take them. 'Cath and Barshin the shoemakers,' he said. 'Well done. You should set up a shop. Call it "A Load of Old Cobblers". But they're no good to me. Only those who destroyed the real boots could bring them back, and I believe that was Cath and someone else.'

'Yes,' said Cath. 'It was Danny and me. I made the left one. He made the right.'

Sammael snorted. 'If you expect me to believe that . . .'

Cath thrust the boots towards him. 'We went into Chromos and killed Zadoc.'

'*You* might have. But I'd bet anything that Danny O'Neill didn't.'

Cath shrugged. 'It's true, though. We went into Chromos, and we wanted the boots back. Both of us – him and me. So we got them. They won't disappear. They're yours.'

Still Sammael refused to take them. 'Danny O'Neill wouldn't have wanted them,' he said. 'I sent him a dog in a million to make him brave, and he was still afraid of me. Where is he now? Cowering in the shadows somewhere?'

'He's gone to take Tom back to Death. And then I think he's going to wait for you to come and kill him,' said Cath. 'Once you've gone into Chromos and given us back our colour again, of course. That's what he wants now, and he's made it happen.'

Sammael stared at her. His face changed colour, from white to pale orange. His eyes flashed a dark red. His hair shone with streaks of emerald and purple, and his shirt was tinged with blue.

He reached out and took the boots in both hands. As he touched them, his whole body trembled, and his mouth opened.

Instead of words, a stream of stars poured from between his lips. Tiny as candle flames, they danced into the winter's night, drifting up the sky and growing in size and brightness as they went.

The stars floated away, as brilliant as bubbles catching at the sun. But these stars caught no light other than their own: they shone with gold as they raced up into the black sky and found places for themselves at the very top of it, blazing across the darkness in a trail of light.

Cath watched them for a moment, and Barshin watched them and Shimny watched them, and each knew that the earth would never be enough for them, now. They had seen the stars set alight to the sky, and it was the beginning of countless new worlds, made from bravery and despair and sheer astonishment. And hope.

By the time Sammael closed his mouth, he had already put the boots on. They had missed the moment of seeing him do it.

He held out his hand to Cath and opened his mouth again, but this time it was only to speak normal words.

'Thank you,' he said. 'They fit well. When I sent Ori, it was my dream to make Danny O'Neill brave enough to return to Chromos and bring out my boots again. I had lost all hope that he would ever do it. But you, it seems, can move mountains.'

Cath took his hand, and the colours of Chromos flooded through her. The gorse over her skin blazed as yellow as a summer's day.

She looked at it in wonder. 'How did you get the sand so fast?' she asked. 'Did you have some left?'

Sammael shook his head. 'I didn't need sand to bring colour back to you. You brought it back to yourself.'

Cath didn't understand. 'What do you mean? I was grey before you shook my hand. Barshin still is. We were dying.'

Sammael reached down and touched the hare. Barshin was brown again, black tips to his ears, a pale smudge under his tail.

'You are the Guardians of Chromos,' said Sammael. 'All three of you. It isn't my doing, don't ask me to change it. It isn't even Chromos who chose you. You chose yourselves.

You watched the stars of my hope fly into the sky, and you wanted nothing but to follow them. You are the wildest of all the creatures – yet you have great hearts. You'll ride over the great plain of Chromos and guide others towards the dreams that they deserve until something stops you, as you stopped Zadoc. But what that thing will be, none of us can predict.'

He turned his fierce eyes on Barshin. 'I still owe you something.'

'But you can't have my sand any more,' said the hare. 'Not if it belongs to Chromos.'

'Even so,' said Sammael. 'I offer you Marija's sand. Where do you want it? Shall I give it to Death, and let her put it back in the earth?'

Barshin was silent for a moment, and then his fur blazed silver in the golden starlight.

'I've seen the world without Chromos,' the hare said. 'And now I am Chromos. And I see what she wanted to be a part of. When I think of her, spinning through the world in a blaze of colour, with Chromos attached to every particle of her – I think that's what she would have wanted. She loved the light and the colour. She loved to leap and jump. And she loved to fight. I never understood exactly what it was that she loved so much. But now I see it. Keep her. I'll never find her again, but she'll be everywhere.'

The hare dipped his silver head, and looked away into the shining darkness. Cath's hand ached to reach out and touch his fur, but she let him be. They would have plenty of time to spend together on the plains of Chromos.

'And you –' Sammael turned to Shimny – 'you have your home already, although I can't take credit for it. That was one good use of that wretched *Book of Shadows* – at least Danny O'Neill wrote you a fine ending.'

'What is it?' asked Shimny. 'I don't know what he wrote.'

'That you would find the best place you ever could have wished for. And you did – your coat changed to red and gold, the colours of your shining heart. You'll find a good home in Chromos.'

'Why did the Earth burn?' asked Cath. 'Did Danny write that, too?'

Sammael shook his head. 'That was my work. I needed the dreams to fight for me, so I took them away. On Earth, dreams often hide inside the shadows, waiting for the right wistful creature to come along and need them. Without them, the shadows grew thin, and the earth began to burn. But that's enough explanations from me. You are all quite healthy looking now, it seems. I had better go and collect my prize, hadn't I?'

'Can't you let him go?' asked Cath. 'He did the bravest thing he could ever do: he made himself understand that you weren't all bad, though you scared him so much. He deserves to get what he wants now, I reckon.'

'Does he?' asked Sammael, raising an eyebrow. 'And what's that?'

'Just . . . the chance to live and die like the rest of them,' said Cath. 'Like a normal human being.'

Sammael curled his lip. 'Don't make me lose hope again,' he said. 'Don't tell me he hasn't changed.'

Cath shrugged. 'Of course he's changed,' she said. 'But not into what you'd want. He doesn't want to be wild and he never will. He's human and he's kind, and I reckon he's the sort of person the Earth needs to be made of. That'd be good for every creature that lives on it. But I guess you'll decide for yourself about that.'

'Do you want to come and say goodbye?' asked Sammael, with a mocking edge to his voice.

Cath shook her head. 'We've already said it,' she said. And she closed her heart.

'Off you go, then,' said Sammael. 'Go and take your places.'

Cath leapt up onto Shimny's back, and Barshin jumped into her arms. None of them weighed anything any more. Cath spread the cloak around her shoulders and narrowed her eyes against the blinding stream of colour that opened up before them. It rose into the sky, a wide and gleaming path, and Shimny's gold hooves began to race along it, sending spray after spray of red and turquoise and yellow and bright jade into the black sky as they lifted and fell. The path was smooth and bright, and the horse put her head down and charged, up into a new world.

On the horse's back, the hare sat balanced, looking forward between the red and gold ears. And the girl sat easily astride, head held high, black hair tangled in the wind. The cloak billowed out behind her, and she felt not a single tinge of regret at leaving the soft old Earth. Onwards, upwards, into Chromos –

The hooves beat out a pattern up the wide path of colours, and the girl smiled.

Chapter 25

After The Storm

High on the hilltop, icy dawn crept into Hangman's Wood. Only the wood itself remembered the day it had been christened, and its name hadn't come from a violent act: no murders had taken place in it; no gibbets had been crafted from its trees. Many centuries before, a tree had been felled by lightning. Thor's hammer, someone had said. And Hammer Wood had gradually become Hangman's.

The gentle wood had never thought that it would wake one day to find the body of a boy lying burnt and broken at the foot of an ancient tree.

Over him stood a man-like creature, as old as the hills and fields, as old as the sky itself. The creature was holding a small book in his hands made from sailcloth and a few ripped scraps of paper. They were singed around the edges, but generally intact; a half-formed scrawl could be seen running across the pages.

'Not bad,' said the creature. 'Not bad for a first attempt. Who knows what could have been?'

The air slipped around the trees, trailing cold behind it as the sun began to stir below the horizon. And Death came walking up the hillside.

'He's mine,' said Sammael.

Death shook her head. 'Look at his eyes.'

The boy's eyes were a soft brown in his charred face. They held determination: a suggestion of the person he might have lived to become.

Sammael gave them a cursory look and nodded. 'You're right,' he said. 'He walked into the storm, into his own death. He got away from me.'

There was no trace of anger in his voice. Death frowned. 'Just like that? You agree?'

Sammael put his head on one side, still contemplating the boy. 'Plenty more fish in the sea,' he said. 'I'll take the ones who want to swim with me. The taro's been taken back by the storm. He's no threat to me any more. You can put him back where he wants to be.'

'He doesn't want anything,' said Death. 'He's dead. Thanks to you.'

Sammael nodded. 'He'd prefer being in the earth to being with me, though.'

'He'd prefer to be alive,' said Death, stooping to gather up the boy. 'Shame you couldn't have left him that as an option. But I'll take care of him, now.'

Sammael looked up at the last of his stars as the gathering day stole them from the sky. When he looked down again,

Death's back was turned, and she was beginning to walk away.

'Wait!' he called.

Death turned, sighing. 'What now?'

Sammael pointed to the east, in the direction of the rising sun. From the edge of the trees, a stag stepped delicately into the half-light, his antlers silhouetted against the sky. As he approached, the hairs of his red-brown coat stood out auburn in the sun's first rays, but there was silver around his muzzle and grey through his haunches.

'Do not come closer,' said Death. 'The living should not approach me.'

'I am not here to approach you,' said the stag. 'I am here to vouch for his courage.'

And from between the stag's hooves a cat slipped into the daylight, sleepily blinking through grey tabby fur. She sat down, licked a paw and yawned.

'I'm only a cat,' she said. 'But I suppose if I've got to vouch for something, I'd say he is a friend of mine. I make no other particular claims.'

From behind the stag's antlers, two birds flew out, although they should have been thousands of miles away, bathing in sunshine. The swallows fluffed up their feathers against the freezing dawn.

'We are freedom,' they said. 'We are the freedom of the heart, to love what it pleases. We say that his heart loved us, and the world, just as it is.'

The small band of creatures rested together, looking at Death with hope in their eyes.

'It seems,' said Sammael, 'that there are a few creatures who don't want that boy to die.'

'Not many,' said Death. 'There are always mourners at funerals. I can't do anything more about it.'

'But I can,' said Sammael. 'These creatures belong to me, now. They gave themselves to me, and I'll give all of them to you, in exchange for him.'

'What's the use of that?' asked Death. 'You won't be able to bring him back to life either.'

Sammael held up the sailcloth book. 'You did, once. With something very much like this. The covers have gone back to the storm, but the pages of a book contain its life, don't they?'

And his face was neither smiling nor sad. It gave away none of his thoughts.

Death breathed in the sharp air of the new day, and it seemed to fill her tired old body with a flash of solidness.

'Take him,' she said. 'I don't want his friends either. If you want to give their sand to anyone, give it to him. Give him dreams of cats and stags and swallows. I only want peace, and I wish the same for all the world's creatures. He's yours.'

'But only on loan,' said Sammael. 'One day, when he needs to die, I'll forsake him. I'll give him to you.'

'And I'll take him,' agreed Death. 'Until then, he's in your hands.'

'Oh, I'll look after him,' said Sammael. And he tore up the sailcloth and the paper with all the scribbles on it, stuffed the bunch of scraps systematically down the throat of Danny O'Neill, and straightened up.

Nodding curtly to the stag, cat and swallows, he slipped back between the trees just as the burning orange sun slipped above the far hills and sent out a ray of yellow light that fell over the blackened corpse.

Danny's charred skin dissolved away back into smooth flesh, as his friends stood over him and watched keenly for the moment he might begin to stir.

Epilogue

Danny chucked his bike down next to the others and made his way up the path between the trees. He heard them before he saw them: they must be in the clearing already.

Laughter. Scuffling. The ping of air-gun pellets hitting tin cans, and clattering, and more laughter.

He flopped down beside them, feeling the earth cold under his belly. Early spring, still. It would soon warm up.

'Hey, Danny. Want a go?'

He took the air gun and aimed it at the rebuilt stack, careful to keep both eyes open, and aimed for the lowest middle can. The pellet struck dead centre, and the stack came crashing down.

He gave a lopsided grin and passed the pistol back. Of course he'd hit it. He never missed. For some reason he couldn't fathom, after all those years of being useless at football, he'd discovered he had a better aim than any of the others.

Saturdays in the woods. He'd go home filthy, and his parents wouldn't mind. Sometimes they caught themselves looking at each other, but what more was there to say? At least now, when they caught each other looking, they smiled.

Two nights ago, there'd been a storm. Danny had woken in the middle of the night and wandered downstairs to have a look at it. He'd found his dad in the kitchen making cocoa. Still in his pyjamas.

Danny raised an eyebrow. His dad took the cocoa upstairs. Back to bed.

The storm had broken the cold edge off the end of winter. Green shoots were beginning to break through the forest floor. Danny brushed his palm over a tiny frond as someone else lined up with the air gun. It was a girl with long, dark hair, messy in the wind.

Not Cath, though. He knew where Cath was now. He saw her everywhere – in the new shoots of spring, in the breaks of weather, in the stones and the streams and the starlight.

What had she written in *The Book of Shadows*? He knew that too. She had left her secret inside the pages, and the pages were in his blood.

He stretched his arms wide across the earth, and for a second he felt it rounding up beneath him, as though the back of a giant animal lay under the soil.

Or as though the whole world were squashing itself into his arms.

He laid his cheek on it and listened to it breathing.

After a while, someone offered him the air gun again. He shook his head.

'I'm on my way home. Got to go to my cousin's memorial service.'

'Your cousin died?'

Raised eyebrows. Awkward silence.

Danny smiled. 'It was a while ago. Everyone's happy to remember him. He was a great guy.'

Nods.

'See you Monday, then.'

'See you.'

He made his way back down the path, peering through the trees. As the sounds of human voices faded and the birdsong rose to claim the air, he heard a rustling to the left, and slowed his steps.

The deer were there. Hinds, fawns, and at their head –

A stag with silver in his coat.

Danny watched for a moment. The stag raised his antlered head.

And watched him back.

Acknowledgements

Thanks to my wonderful agent, Becky Bagnell, my editors Jenny Jacoby and Kate Farrell, Sara O'Connor for making it all possible, all at Hot Key and Henry Holt who've seen these manuscripts through to publication, and the countless inspiring friends who've seen me through the whole Book of Storms trilogy. Special thanks this time to Nicolantonio Prentosito, who named Ori for me, and who knows what the longer version of her name is. And lastly, so many thanks to L, L & S.

Ruth Hatfield

Ruth Hatfield is from Cambridge, although she travels around a bit as she is a field archaeologist by profession. It's a good job for inspiration! Ruth has been writing stories for most of her life just to please herself, however, what she loves to explore is the way in which imagination gives us limitless possibilities to make our own lives extraordinary. In her spare time she eats books, gallops around on horses, pedals around on her bike and tries not to break too many bones.

Discover more in
The Book of Storms
trilogy . . .

Danny alone, must confront his
fears, find his parents, and unravel
the secrets of The Book of Storms.

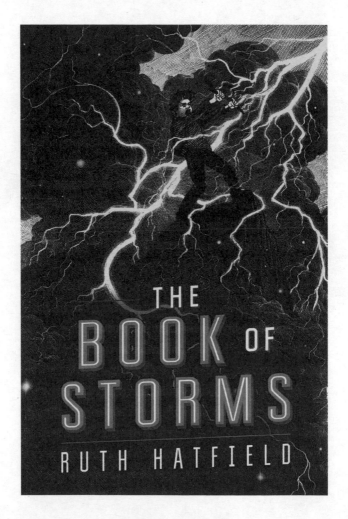

BOOK ONE
Available now

The journey to Chromos is a
dangerous mission, and Danny and
Cath will have to muster every scrap
of bravery and ingenuity to survive.

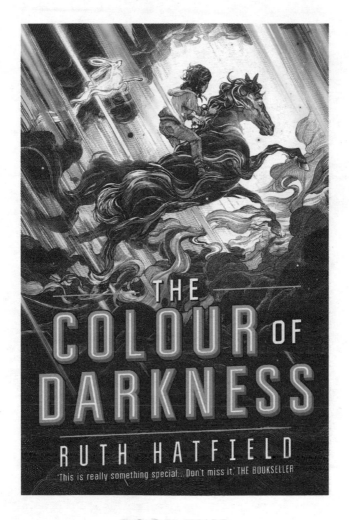

BOOK TWO
Available now

HOT
KEY
BOOKS

Thank you for choosing a Hot Key book.

If you want to know more about our authors
and what we publish, you can find us online.

You can start at our website

www.hotkeybooks.com

And you can also find us on:

We hope to see you soon!